About the Author

Haya Hallak, visual artist and novelist. Born in 1994 in Ariha, Syria. I speak English in addition to Arabic. I live in forced displacement.

The Death of Farah

Haya Hallak

The Death of Farah

Olympia Publishers
London

www.olympiapublishers.com
OLYMPIA PAPERBACK EDITION

Copyright © Haya Hallak 2022

The right of Haya Hallak to be identified as author of
this work has been asserted in accordance with sections 77 and 78
of the Copyright, Designs and Patents Act 1988.

All Rights Reserved

No reproduction, copy or transmission of this publication
may be made without written permission.
No paragraph of this publication may be reproduced,
copied or transmitted save with the written permission of the
publisher, or in accordance with the provisions
of the Copyright Act 1956 (as amended).

Any person who commits any unauthorised act in relation to
this publication may be liable to criminal
prosecution and civil claims for damage.

A CIP catalogue record for this title is
available from the British Library.

ISBN: 978-1-80074-619-0

This is a work of fiction.
Names, characters, places and incidents originate from the writer's
imagination. Any resemblance to actual persons, living or dead, is
purely coincidental.

First Published in 2022

Olympia Publishers
Tallis House
2 Tallis Street
London
EC4Y 0AB

Printed in Great Britain

Dedication

To my novelist mother, Ibtisam Tracy… a mother and a beacon.

Acknowledgements

I would like to thank my father, the novelist Abdul Rahman Hallak, who kindly gave me his valuable comments on the novella. Also, all thanks to the English teacher Absi Albo for his accurate linguistic review. I also spread my deep thanks to my friends, Hassan Al-Khoja and Aws Ezzi, for their continuous support.

-1-

No sooner had I arrived in Istanbul than I called my friend Nariman and told her that I needed some place to stay that night until I could find a good hotel room to rent. She answered me politely: "My sister Farah is in a neighborhood near to Taksim, and she will meet you and help you with everything you need."

It was not my first time walking an Istiklal street, and it wasn't my first time either sitting alone at Arada restaurant. From the first time I visited Istanbul I felt a sense of intimacy between me and that restaurant as well as with Istiklal street due to the distinctive flavor of food belonging to the former, and the over-crowdedness related to the latter. Even though previously I used to hate the crowded places, the warm weather during the whole year, the warmth that wafted out of the gathering of the family around the dining table, my grandmother and my grandfather who gave the long cold nights their intimacy and specialty, the cherry grove where we spent our days from the beginning of spring till the end of the season of quince, pomegranate and walnut, these things were what distinguished my hometown from other parts of the world.

More interestingly, at that time even if we wanted to have a meal at a restaurant in the mountain, we used to choose a corner away from the noise, where we could enjoy watching the plain, the night with its sparkling stars and the serenity that dominated the peaceful sleeps of the city. Once again, overcrowding was one of the reasons that alienated me from big cities and pushed me to live away from pollution, noise, heavy traffic and high prices.

Now I feel that serenity and isolation have become the memories of a past that sometimes presses on my chest robustly and prevents me from breathing easily. Actually, it is not the past only, but my adenoids as well suffocate me.

Though the place implies for the visitors that they are just in a train station, the travelers rotate on the chairs for a few hours, except that for me it is warm and intimate, maybe because of the Armenian waitress. I feel lucky she's always there whenever I go up to the second floor and gives me a wild smile. I feel of it like a vast white snowy space snows on my heart in the hot days, and I salute her with the only word I learned from her mother tongue.

The Armenians in the country that ditched me are a major component in Aleppo. They lived in Syria as if Syria was their own country due to the good treatment they received from the Syrians. More specifically, the Armenians used to gather and live in a very known place called Al Kaydoon when they first fled to Syria and owned their own neighborhoods with time. Besides, the Armenians were highly welcome by the Syrians because of several reasons. First, they were receptive to the new environment and open minded to the new lifestyle. Second, they were hardworking and ambitious in such a way that they were specialized in some careers which met the needs of the Syrian people, such as repairing cars and the gold industry.

Unlike the Armenians living in Syria, in Turkey, their

situation is different because of the historical hostility between the Turkish and the Armenians. Hardly had I come here when I realized how people felt when the society treated them, starting from racial factors which became worse and worse with the risen number of racists in communities with high numbers of refugees who fled the wars and the political persecution in their countries.

Norma came to me to ask in Turkish, with a special accent, what I would like to eat. Without allowing me to answer, she continued saying "as usual, Her Zamanki Gibi." Norma knew what I loved the most because I came here a lot, and I had never changed my food once.
    Finally, Farah came.
    It was not the first time I had seen Farah. I had already visited her at her house in 2014. When the organization I used to work with shut down, I had been searching for jobs or a scholarship that could move me to a safer place at that time. I hoped I could register and enroll in a Turkish university, but I did not match the terms of the scholarship and I could not afford to pay the university bills.

Both I and Farah had some likes more than dislikes, and we shared the same birthday month on the same year as well. But she got married at a young age and gave birth to her daughter when she was eighteen years old. When we first met, I could not recognize Farah's face features. They were always vague and confusing in my mind, and they were not paired to her name when someone mentioned it in front of me. The name seemed strange to me as she was, but what was stranger to me was that I knew her daughter's face by heart, and more than that, I remembered her features while she was one month old and how she changed when she became one year old and then to three to four and so on… the most surprising thing was I remembered how she changed eyes colors, how her hair got longer and thicker, and what she was wearing, those small joyful clothes, some with colored ruffles, the hair ties, her hair arches with the smooth pearls on it, the bracelets and the shoes. All that was very confusing to me, and trying so hard to keep it from Farah, that was why I could not ask her about her daughter since she came alone.

Years ago, I visited her at her place. She had a huge comfortable house, and the furniture was new regardless of being an old European style. I sat on the purple couch in front of a window that took the whole wall. The widow was large enough to fill the whole room with light during the whole day. I was confused and shy as usual and did not know how to start a nice conversation with her until she started talking about the work with the humanitarian organizations, favoritisms, thefts and the ways the people working for the organizations violate the laws. After that, Farah kept speaking about how it's hard to live in a country where the people were bothered by the presence of Syrians and treated them in a racist way. Finally, she spoke about killing and raping for stupid and illogical reasons, about homesickness, nostalgia and remembering the happy old times and missing figs and olives…

Farah sighed and started telling me about a story that happened once to her in Idleb at the beginning of revolution:

"While talking about the olive and the oil, my first - and last demonstration for sure - I was walking back from school with my colleagues at the end of the day. At that day, we heard some girls cheering Bashar Al Assad and cursing

us. I felt outraged, felt the blood bombing to my head and my veins, which were more likely to explode. I ran to them and slapped someone on her face. That day, military members and caps raided our house and took me to the military security branch:

"Are you aware of what you have already done?"

Much worse, before I recognized what the officer was saying, I had fainted after he smacked my face. I twiddled the blood on my clothes while looking at my father rushing into the room crying and begging the officer to leave me. He decided to turn a blind eye from the slap I gave his daughter on one condition: my father had to give him the whole olive oil season in return. Five hundred virgin olive oil tanks he took from my father for setting me free and canceling his daughter's request of killing me."

Farah ordered food for us from a nearby Turkish restaurant. It was super-hot, and it almost killed my taste cells. It was my habit to keep myself away from chilly food because it caused me a kind of allergy. My body suffered a lot from eating capsicum and black pepper. No sooner had I started tasting food than Farah saw the sweat drops that started drooling on my forehead, and the tears that my eyes shed. She laughed:

"I was supposed to ask before if you do not like chilly food. I forgot, I thought you were from Salqin, the same as me. The people in Salqin are famous for eating the chilly capsicum. More specifically, when the season comes, they decorate the balconies with clenched threads of capsicum hanged on the windows like necklaces, while the capsicum paste trays are aligned on the house's rooftops.

It happened once while the mayor was visiting during

the capsicum season, he thought that people decorated their houses celebrating his visit. You surely knew that he was from the coast."

Farah stretched over the table to shake hands:

"I wish you had a safe travel; it has been a long time since I last saw you."

She turned around the table, hugged me warmly, kissed me on the cheeks, and then pulled a chair and sat beside me.

Farah was a girl full of joy. You could see that through her ability to laugh, mock and imitate other people, the way she walked and moved. She rushed while walking in such a way that you would think she was always in a hurry, and unconsciously while talking she gave hints that something really dangerous was keeping her mind busy, or that there was something about to happen and no one could predict it, but her.

She was considered to be tall when compared to her generation. Of all the families I knew, and my family included, mothers are taller than their daughters and their bodies are less flawless and more beautiful! What I really liked about Farah's face the most was her straight nose as if she had a rhinoplasty. Her medium skin was pure and shiny, and her black veil gave her more purity.

The way Farah wore her veil showed boredom, laziness and rejection. I asked her why she wouldn't take it off as long as she wore it carelessly, and the cloth was so smooth to an extent that it fell off every now and then and in a lazy way she pulled it back again.

Farah called our friend Rima, who asked us not to order coffee until she arrived, and that she needed fifteen minutes to join us.

Rima's beautiful face with her white pure skin and eyes

colored with the spectra of dark green and her long blond hair disclosed her Roman origins who lived in the Al Bara area which was obviously characterized with two things: 'the ancient pyramids', and 'white hair and eyelashes, red skin, and colored eyes with green and mostly blue.'

Farah:

"Rima looks like a teenager; she never grows old. By the way, what age do you think she is?"

"Maybe in her twenties."

"No, in her thirties..."

They laughed... I smiled worriedly. I knew Rima's age in spite of her continuous efforts to hide it. We were together at high school and again at university, and she always claimed that she was younger than us though no one asked her age. Accidentally, I discovered that Rima was five years older than me... she told me when she got her secret revealed that once when she was a child, she got sick, and she was forced to fall behind in school by the doctor's order. And she told other girls that she was carrying her elder sister's name who died in a car accident and that her mother refused to adjust her name in the birth certificate. And once, she told us that her father told her uncle to register her, who in his turn wrote her birthday date wrong...

Her interesting stories stayed part of her personality, which no one held her accountable for, because her features said that she was way younger than the birth date recorded on her ID.

Rima was born in January, and she is a Capricorn just like me! And this is considered to be the thrilling fact that gathered the three of us. We were in a harmonious mood that not only stars, but also destinations connect us with a similar fate, as always did Farah insist on.

We ordered Turkish tea... Farah was not much into tea 'submissively'. She told me once that she loves it with jasmine aroma served in Chinese porcelain cups that her grandfather brought once from one of his visits to China, which her grandmother kept in a glass cupboard filled with delicately made crochet toppers. The cup sets never left their place unless there was a very important guest. Farah's grandfather was a very well-known trader; he was one of the richest men in our hometown, and his father was Aga... inherited money and lands. Nevertheless, he spent all it "while he was alive" - as they say – on traveling. He used to say, "if God loved his servant, He shows him what He owns", and his belief made him enjoy his life and guaranteed the love of the Creator.

The waiter brought the tea...

I drank it alone, Rima ordered coffee. She wanted Farah to read it for her as usual. She insisted on reading her cup whenever we met. I have a weird feeling that Farah took advantage of that chance to take revenge on Rima and tell her the bad and ugly things her cup showed. And that was how she felt superior and fed on her friend's feeling of refraction.

She moved the coffee cup in circular motions, turned it on the tray, then said:

"We have to wait now for a while."

We sat quietly without saying a word until Farah held the cup again and said:

"You will travel, but not inside Turkey. It will be out of the country, but it may take three to five years."

She flipped the cup to another side and said:

"The one you are in love with now will leave you soon, for him you are just a time to kill and a void to fulfill. He is playing with your emotions, and your problems at work won't be solved, you will quit and start searching for a new job…"

Secretly I smiled. It was normal that she knew all these pieces of information about her!

Every time we gathered; Rima became more obsessed with drinking bitter coffee. She flipped her cup with a weird surrender and waited for Farah's words as if she would be led to the guillotine. The blood bumped into her face, she lost her concentration, and she couldn't breathe easily until Farah had finished her talk with Rima's "fingerprint" in the bottom of the coffee cup ("there are problems between your sister and her husband, they will get divorced soon").

Farah looked me straight in the eyes and said:

"Why are you afraid of reading your cup? I am sure that you never drink coffee every time we meet, so I cannot read your cup. But guess what, **I drank my cup this time intending it for you.**"

I smiled hardly:

"It won't work. You know it is not about intentions, the cup has to be mine and I should drink it. Do not circumvent me, I will not believe a word you say."

"Try me this time, you won't lose anything."

She held the cup, looked carefully, and said:

"There is a scorpion in your cup, it entered your land not long ago and it will sting you right at the moment you are expecting it to. You won't be able to stop it."

She looked at me, smiled and continued:

"Your grandmother is tired. I see that she might go through a surgery or maybe she already does. Your cup says she will go back to Syria soon."

I told myself, okay, maybe that is something no one but

my family knows, maybe she can really read… she continued:

"There is a book in your back bag."

I answered with a smile:

"True, I am reading 'After the Quake' for Haruki Murakami."

She continued:

"You will travel far away but not now; your cup says that you are about to apply for a scholarship but do not put your hopes in it; they will not choose you."

I felt completely shocked due to the fact that she just mentioned three things no one knew, and do I have really to lose my faith in the scholarship? How could she see such a thing in a coffee cup? Impossible, I looked at her amazed and quickly I took the cup from her and looked into it. There was the scorpion in the bottom of the cup, dancing counterclockwise. I started to lose my vision and felt the place start to dance along with the scorpion.

I held my head not to fall. Farah stood and held my face with both hands and asked if I was feeling good… I said:

"I feel a little bit dizzy, maybe, because of traveling and smoking."

Rima:

"We can go to my house whenever you want."

I said:

"We can have one last teacup and cigarette and we are fine to go."

Money was not a problem at that time as I could pay the bill whatever it was, my salary was really good. After paying, we went out to take a cap. The weather was nice and warm with chilly and humid breeze. We arrived at Rima's place in Akyol Street almost at half past eleven. Her apartment was small; two rooms and a bathroom, a bedroom and a sitting room that opened on a small kitchen, but it was cozy and enough for a person living by themselves. She gave me a pajama to change, we smoked some cigarettes while talking about my exam the next morning, then she gave me a blanket and a pillow and opened the couch to sleep on after insisting on me to sleep in the bedroom. But I don't love to make anyone uncomfortable. That's why I chose the couch.

I had to prepare myself for a month before the IELTS exam, so I could apply for scholarships in Europe and the US, but this time was easier since it wasn't my first time to do the exam. I thought, I don't have to prepare myself intensely. It was my only dream at that time to attend the university and continue my studies and then to get a master in the field of monitoring and evaluation or humanitarian work, high hopes it was, and I planned for myself everything that might happen and want to do in the future. I thought they would accept me in the scholarship, and I would move to the US and live with Niel, and after continuing my study, we may move to Turkey or South Africa to work with humanitarian organizations. I was a naive kid, because, deep down inside, I didn't know that life doesn't offer us what we want to have in the way we want it to be. That's why I gave the priority to the imaginary dreams and pinky love. I should have gone after study for my love for it instead of being captivated by unrequited or one-sided love.

Since change takes place from time to time, my desire has unexpectedly changed after a while to start applying for Political Science instead of humanitarian aid.

I woke exhausted the next morning. I looked myself in the mirror and my eyes were puffy and had the dark circles underneath them because of exhaustion and smoking. Then, I got my tooth brush out of the traveling back and went to the bathroom to wash my face, got my clothes out and wore them and boiled some water for coffee when I saw Rima coming out of her room yawning, exhausted as I was. We excessively drank coffee together and I started to feel the exam anxiety in my stomach. Much worse, my forehead started to sweat, and I got freezing fingers. I started to console myself by saying it's an easy thing and I'm good at it anyway, to calm myself down before I went. Rima had given me a copy of her key…

I went out, stopped a taxi, and told him about my destination. I arrived at the Renaissance Hotel in Besiktas at half past eight and went to the security man to ask him where the exam hall was. He informed me that it was downstairs, but I had to wait for a while in the hotel hall until they called for us. Half an hour, it was almost like half a year for me. I felt dizzy and had stomachache because of the stress and not having had breakfast. The waiting hall was a medium size one full of students and among them there were a few hotel residents. You could differentiate them from the way they sat, relaxed and quiet, busy reading a newspaper or sideway conversations.

We had to finish a few things before entering the exam hall. I put all my stuff and the phone in a specific place. Furthermore, I had to hand them my passport so they could have a copy and then stand in front of a camera to take a picture to put it on the results certificate. At **that specific moment**, I remembered the time I stood in front of the camera in the Emniyet NarlIca two days after I fled Idleb to take a picture to put it on the refugee ID. I was so confused at that time, following the policeman's instructions who was taking the photo for me. I wasn't one of those who loved to take pictures, especially formal ones. In my opinion photos are for beautiful girls and I didn't consider myself to be one.

The cop told me to put all my fingers one after another on the laser machine to take my fingerprints and then continued saying: "you can come tomorrow to receive your IDs." I hated the fact that I was forced to get an ID to stay here, or even to be defined as a refugee, and I was sure then that I wasn't going back to Syria again. I felt my face falling and my soul changed...

Next day, I went again to the Emniyet department to receive my ID card. Now I was officially a refugee in Turkey, who didn't have a house, a job, or even money, and who couldn't continue her study. For not one day have I stopped trying to get revenge for that girl with small easy dreams; to help them come true for any human being living in a country where they respect his humanity.

The exam was four sections: listening, writing, reading and speaking. I had to take the first three tests in the hotel and for the speaking I had to take it in the British cultural center the next day.

I felt so relieved after finishing the first day tests. I had only speaking left, and for me it was so easy, for it was the speaking language skill that I developed in my workplace through the last two years until now.

When I came back home, I found Rima awake. She asked me if I was hungry, I nodded "yes...", she brought cheese toasts for both of us with two cups of tea and asked me if I had a desire to go out. I said, "honestly, I don't like staying inside doors and prefer to spend most of my time out." She smiled without commenting. We finished the toasts, she went to her room to get ready, and then gave me her mascara to put some on, saying: "You look pale."

We went out and walked the way to Cihangir. I was fond off the place. I loved Tophane, I loved Karakoy, and I loved Cihangir the most. There were so many trees on both sides of the way, and when we arrived at the main street of Cihangir, we walked around the cafes, restaurants and bars until we chose Bi alt kat restaurant located immediately in front of Kemel Orhan's house, which became a museum after his death.

Rima ordered a beer, and in two minutes she left me to go to the bathroom. The waiter came to me and asked if I could give him Rima's number. I answered in English with some Turkish words that I could not, and that he could ask her in person. I loved that moment knowing how to speak Turkish, it was a funny situation. When she came back, I talked to her about the 'In Jail with Nazim Hikmet' novel. Most surprisingly, I read in 2015 the story about the period of time Nazim and Kemel spent in jail during the communism spread. It was obvious that she didn't know who they are, but she was really into the conversation. Then I said: "We can visit Kemel's house if you want. There it is in front of us." She was excited about going there. Another museum, near where we were, was called Museum of Innocence, owned by the writer Orhan Bamuk. She said: "We can visit it later."

Orhan Kemel's museum was his own house. It was two floors, and you could see in the first-floor pictures of his family and friends. Also, some of his writings were printed and hanged on the walls, while the upper floor was his bedroom and his office at the same time. There was a small bed, a library full of books, and in the corner a statue wearing Kemal's clothes, and there was as well a small green table with some sheets of paper on it, some photos hanged on the wall and a big wooden closed box.

Hardly had we finished when we came back home to have some rest till the evening. Then, we gathered again with Farah in Arada restaurant, and as usual we sat in the back yard near to the kitchen. The smell of pizza coming from the kitchen was delicious. As usual, we sat in the corner and Farah asked me how I did in the exam. I told her it was not hard, but I still have the speaking test and I will finish. She wished me luck while Rima interrupted her saying:

"I cannot handle my workplace anymore, some people are prattlers by nature, they cannot stop gossiping about each other in a gross way, also the salary is not enough at all, and I could not market the hair planting and surgeries perfectly."

I told her she had to quit her job; if she was not comfortable with what she was doing she would not be able to give her best. She agreed by nodding her head. Farah looked at me and said:

"We have to introduce you to Diana, Rima's sister."

I felt awkward, I didn't like meeting new people because I was a shy person, and for that I do not know how to start a conversation with them. But I agreed to meet her, what harm could that do? Rima was almost like me when it came to talking to strangers. That is why I did not suffer spending time with her, we did not have to talk when we did not want to, and we felt comfortable for that. I wondered how could Diana's personality be, and could I adapt to her? Was she older or younger? I didn't ask...

This time we stayed for a longer time at the restaurant, until one o'clock. I couldn't stop yawning since it was eleven p.m., though I was enjoying my time a lot and I didn't want to go home. I felt that I luckily found a second family here in Istanbul, but I couldn't keep my eyes open any longer since I woke up very early that day, and we had to go back home. Farah insisted on me taking a nap, so I could stay up late.

I was not stressed the way I was yesterday. For me, talking is much easier than anything else, and the exam was not early; it was at eleven o'clock so I could sleep more.

Next day, I went to the exam center, the British Cultural Center, to have the conversation part. A worker there led me to the room where I was supposed to take my exam. I entered the room; it was more like a classroom. More definitely, there were three rounded tables with two or three chairs around. Besides, there was a white board and a small cupboard full of envelopes and papers.

My interviewer asked me to sit on the chair next to the table. She sat behind. She was medium height, curvy, her hair was neither log nor short; it was black and curly, and her eyes were black like a dark night. She seemed mid her forties. Her quiet smile and kindness made me feel comfortable and we started talking. On the surface, everything was smooth and went the same way I wanted it to, until she asked the last question, saying:

"Tell me about a site you visit frequently? Who told you about it? And what is it about?"

I forgot everything.

I started cracking and playing with my fingers. I was so nervous, and for a moment I didn't know what was happening anymore. Much worse, my brain stopped working like an old computer. I could have talked about sites and applications I was using daily at my work in monitoring and evaluation, however my mind limited my options to choose only one site which I couldn't talk about for a long time, unfortunately, because I wasn't the one using it, it was Rima.

I talked for a while about it, but I couldn't continue talking for a longer period of time. I was really upset, I wished I could change places with Rima; then I could continue talking without stopping, without straying and stuttering.

The lady said:

"You can leave now; I wish you luck."

I thanked her and went out, taking my back bag and my passport. I got out of the building, I didn't want to take a cap, I walked along Besiktas way until I arrived at Findikli. To my great surprise, all the way there I was remembering Farah's daughter's beautiful face; such remembrance made me feel at peace.

Rima was waiting for me when I arrived. She wanted to go out, and I didn't want to stay home either while I was in Istanbul. As usual we went out walking to Cihangir, but this time we chose the Teas Café - weird, ha! This is what Syrians there used to call it. The real name was Kardeşler; it was four cafes beside each other, though there were no borders in between, owned by Istanbul municipality, and located on the corner of a crossroads of Cihangir main street, and it served cheap tea. There was another cafe beside these cafes which was called Firuz.

We sat outside waiting for Farah. When she arrived, we asked the waiter to bring us tea in broken Turkish. He said, "You can talk to me in Arabic." Farah asked:

"Where are you from?"

"I'm Syrian, from Homs."

A wide smile full of happiness appeared on Farah's face, and she said:

"It's an honor… what's your name?"

"Moustafa."

"You're welcome, Moustafa, I'm Farah."

Moustafa went to the kitchen to bring us tea and went back to his work.

I was dreaming about moving and living in Istanbul since I was in tenth grade. I hated school at that time and that was because my best friend moved to another school and other girls used to bully me. I used to feel that they were more beautiful than me, which made me lose my confidence. That was the reason that affected my study negatively. At that time, I was living at my grandmother's house. After I had come back home pretending to finish my studies, I used to come to the living room to watch Turkish series'. Istanbul was mysteriously vague to me. I usually picture it cloudy and rainy, maybe because most of the series used to be filmed in winter. But my fondness of Istanbul never weakened my longing to Antakya.

I was so attached to Antakya because there was a weird connection, especially with the house we were renting in Cumhuriyet Street. Our house was duplex. I lived with my grandmother and relatives. My room was the one upstairs with a small bathroom and a balcony overseeing the house roofs of Antakya where I used to see the brick, wet with rainwater.

In my room, there was a special corner for my paintings and a small table full of colors and the canvas easel. Near to it there were three home plant pots. My bed was small, covered with yellow blankets - yellow is my favorite color - while my closet was a big one left by the house owner. There was a very small white closet inside the wall, and beside it there was a small library full of books and small statues, while in the middle there was a table on which there was my laptop, a sketch notebook, a small notebook, fruit plates and a water bottle. Before I went to sleep, I used to light a candle and put it on the ground because I fear darkness.

When I woke up in the morning, I always imagined my room overviewing the sea because of the sound of the strong breeze that moved the curtains instantly. I loved my room so much and it was another reason that kept me wondering if I really wanted to move to Istanbul… that is the curse of feeling strongly attached to places. For that, I'm a person with screwy heart that can't afford separation, even if it wasn't my own house; maybe because I always put a part of my soul in it and became afraid of leaving it. Every time I change a house, my soul gets weaker… a few years were enough to feel that she was going to abandon me soon, I felt from the way I received the news of death, destruction and absence…

The third reason was that Mariyam wasn't just a friend, she was a piece of my heart, or something else I don't know exactly what, but she used to captivate me in a magical way. I didn't understand for one day my strong attachment to her, and I can't for one moment picture my life without her. Also, my job was one of the strongest causes.

Slowly, the sound of Farah's laugh brought me back while she was saying:

"Lucky guy, the one you're thinking about."

With a smile, I answered:

"My grandmother's face."

A sense of quietness reigned before she asked:

"And when are you going to move here and live between us?"

I answered:

"Maybe soon. I'm not sure, and maybe never… my plane

leaves tomorrow morning, but I'm coming back soon for a meeting with my manager."

"Then you can stay at my place next time."

"I would be happy to."

In the evening, I packed my bag in preparation to go back to Antakya the next day. As usual, we sat, me and Rima talking and smoking cigarettes before going to sleep. She said:

"I think you're tired, we don't have to stay up late tonight."

We smoked the last cigarette and went to sleep.

Next morning, I went to Taksim Square to take the Havaş bus that would drive me to the airport. The driver's assistant approached me and said: "on üç" thirteen Turkish Lira for the bus ticket. I gave him the money, and wore my headphones, hoping that music would make me not only pass the time more quickly but also forget about the road distance. I always had this weird feeling on the traveling road. As far as travelling for long distances is concerned, I often feel that something big might happen and I would not find a way to deal with it.

Luckily, I arrived at Ataturk airport safely and went to the checkpoint. As soon as I had finished, I headed to take my ticket. Then, I stepped forward, waiting until my turn came. I gave the employee my passport. She looked at me carefully and nodded to a policeman to come to her. From her body language, I understood that she asked whether I'm the same girl in the passport or not. He answered, "yes, but she's 'kapali'"- it means wearing Hijab but literally means 'closed'. She gave the ticket to me and told me in a broken English that I needed to head to the gate because soon the plane would take off. When the time came for the plane to take off, I relaxed in my seat and felt my soul flying above. It was my favorite moment. I tried to read few pages when the plane had gone on a straight track... but still I was sleepy, so I decided to take a nap. To my great surprise, I slept until I heard the captain saying: "we will be landing in ten minutes". As much as I loved the minute the plane takes off, I hated waiting for the luggage. I used to tell myself, if my bag came within the first ten, I'll be lucky with something on my mind, but it always came late or even the last one, though I bought it yellow just for them to notice it.

As usual, the first thing I do when I arrive, I put my bag at home and went to see Marie at Kuş Café. Every time I went out of my home, I saw my barber neighbor sitting out of his shop on a small wooden chair drinking tea. I remembered my grandfather every time I saw him. I headed down town, down the street until I reached Asi river. The smell emitting from the dry river suffocated me, and the mosquitoes bit me until I crossed the river and İnönü Street coming after, and then to hürriyet Street. I walked the avenue watching the compacted restaurants and clothes shops till I reached the end of it, where most of the silk scarf shops that Antakya is famous for were located. From that place, I went right entering Asi Street, a few steps, and I arrived at my destination. The café is an entrance for a closed arcade, so small. There were three tables and on each one there were two benches for four people. Sometimes, Marie and I had to leave our things and go to the closest restaurant to use the toilet, because there was no one in our favorite café. The café owner was a close friend of Marie. Out of kindness, he once took us in his car to his grandmothers' land. It was small and full of Kiwi and berry trees with a house, small and dilapidated from the outside. We ate and went out again to St. Simon Manastiri to the south west of Antakya, almost about twenty-nine kilometers away. It was the remains of a monastery, and next to it there was a huge windmill. The scene was captivating in such a way that during the sunset you felt on the edge of the world.

Here, Marie arrived with the most beautiful smile you could ever see, shouting from the entrance:

Canim, I missed you. We should sit, write your motivation letters, finish your application, and send it to the university."

"I'm not optimistic about it, Marie. Colombia University is so majestic and ancient, I won't be the perfect candidate for them."

"Don't say that we have to apply and leave the rest to God. Just remember this; good things always happen at Kuş."

It wasn't true what she said, for that was closer than the eyelash and eyelid to the bad things that were about to happen to me from here. After we had finished applying, Marie asked me:

"Are you talking with Niel?"

I smiled and answered:

"Sometimes we talk."

I met Niel, the country representative, who was responsible for the organization that I started newly to work with on the first day of work. When he entered the room, I couldn't take my eyes away from him. He had deeply got my admiration, so have I. To my surprise, my friends always mocked me when I admired him. We used to go hiking with other colleagues on Sundays. Before I traveled to Istanbul to have the IELTS exam, he had sent me a short message at two a.m. saying, "what do you think about going tomorrow before the sunset for a hike?" Next day, we went together; he was waiting on the other side across the river in front of Hatay

Kunefe restaurant. We crossed streets and the lanes of old Antakya to the way that led us to the hiking point. The weather was very hot. Much worse, humidity was really high as usual, because Antakya was close to the sea; he was four steps ahead of me. Once we finished a quarter of the way, he said:

"Do you know why I did not tell anyone to come with us?"

I answered:

"I know, but I need you to assure me."

He turned to me and said:

"I cannot stop thinking about you."

Sometimes, our way was soil and easy and other times it was bumpy and full of thorns, small shrubs and wildflowers that had not been killed by the hot weather of July. We made our way up to the rock overlooking the whole of Antakya, which he later called his favorite spot. The sun was starting to sleep over Antakya. He said:

"Isn't it beautiful?"

"Yes."

"Or at least up from here."

The city was twinkling like a wide sea from far away. I started to feel that what had been happening was no more than a short dream which might end soon when I woke up, or a daydream like those which used to intrigue me during the math class. My heart beats were like a little child's who'd lost his way home after school, and his laugh was like a kid's laugh on the first days of Eid after wearing their new clothes. His eyes were shimmering like window glass under the morning sun rays… I loved him from the first laugh. When I remember what happened, I realize that it was really a short dream, and I should not have fallen to its vestibules. He was not honest with me. Unfortunately, only two months passed on his confession. He came to surprise me that we had to break up for now because the two of us were working together, and I was naive not to know that he was coward enough not to say the truth.

We walked, Marie and I, almost for two hours in the streets of Antakya after we had got out of Kuş, and after that she took me in her Nissan Vanette, which we called later 'Dove', to her mother's house. This was a little far from the city center in a place called Küçükdalyan. Her father built the house. You could see it was old and tired, but Marie was rebuilding it from her own money. Also, I met her cow Lily…

She said:

"Mom and Dad never eat eggs unless they are from their own chicken and do not drink milk unless it is from our own cow."

She told me once that her mom was in the habit of reading The Holy Quran, but she could not understand most of what she was reading… Her mom was so nice, but she had a very traditional way of thinking. She once loved someone that used to teach with her in the university. They fell in love in a short time, but when she told her mother about him, the mother refused him at once because Marie was Alawite. That was why she should be marrying someone like her.

Marie drove me back home near the evening time. However, I didn't like to stay home. I had gone to my hairdresser friend to have some coffee and chat before I went home. Yamama was forty years old. She was married, but she did not have any kids. She considered me as a sister since the day we met in the year 2016. We started to tell each other about all the things we were going through. Barely had I finished my cup of coffee when I went back home. I suffered too much while going upstairs for being so tired… I changed my clothes and went to the kitchen to prepare a plate of fruits to have while watching one of Hayao Miyazaki's movies. This movie really makes me feel so peaceful and that's what I need it before going to sleep, so I can win the battles that I will have during my sleep.

-2-

With the end of 2017, Kuş Café went bankrupt and lost the trait of being our favorite place, especially after the taste of coffee changed. Slowly, the city started to change, and the number of organizations working there downsized because of not getting authorization from the Turkish government to reopen the offices after the expiration of the previous licenses. I heard rumors then saying that the Turkish government wanted the fund to pass through them and then they gave it to the organizations. We traveled with most of the foreign staff to work from Athena, and that's what made my promotion almost impossible.

During my birthday in the middle of January, I was gifted a new separation. Marie was confused between staying in Antakya or accepting the new offer in Kahramanmaraş that she has always hated. Trying to keep my tears from falling, I advised her to go and accept the new position while my heart was squeezing in pain, but she deserved the best. She looked at me and said:

"I will come to Antakya at the end of every week. Do not worry, and we can spend the time together."

The end of the week was never enough for me. I was so lonely, and Marie was the only one who was able to kill my loneliness. How was it going to be for me after she had gone?

Antakya became empty and bleak like my life in 2018. It

was not a good year at all; bad gifts kept coming even after my birthday had ended. Every time I opened one, I found another nightmare. In February, after renewing my passport that did not allow me to go anywhere except for renewing my Turkish residency, I heard the news of my uncle and his two-and-a-half-year-old daughter's deaths after the missile strikes on Saraqep. My uncle was a father of four children living with his wife and my single aunt in my grandparents' ground house in Saraqep. He was tender and steadfast as a mountain. I remember his face vaguely. When I was a kid, sometimes my mom used to send me to sleep at my grandparents' house. Scarcely had you entered the house when you noticed that there was a vast unroofed yard like the old Arabic houses in the middle. There was a cement basin for plants and the rooms were around the yard. There were four bedrooms, a sitting room, a kitchen and a bathroom, and an additional room on the roof. The roof was really vast. My aunt was considered a little bit tall, skinny, with brown eyes, small nose and a freckled face. They tell me that I look like her, took the shape of the eyes, the hair, the crooked teeth and the freckles. She used to do her very long hair in braids and always tell me: "You should comb your hair under the olive tree, it will get longer." She loved Indian movies and series, and she used to spend the whole evening in front of the TV watching Indian channels. At night, I helped her move the pillows and blankets to the roof in preparation to sleep. I enjoyed looking at the full-of-stars sky when I laid down before sleep, wishing someday I could touch it or know what was going on up there… I wondered if there were other people living outside of our world, and after a short time, I started to see the stars getting inside of each other and sleepiness weighed down my eyelids, as if I were hypnotized.

In the morning, my uncle bought us the soft sweet bread in the shape of a doughnut but bigger, and his wife boiled some milk for breakfast. The bread wasn't so different from the Turkish Açma in shape, but it was way more delicious. In the afternoon, it was so hot my aunt went outside, held the hose and started watering the plans and washing the big jasmine tree, and then cleaned the ground and cut a watermelon for us to eat it.

"There was no body to bury," my aunt said on the phone… "he turned to shreds."

It was not so far, the day that my uncle's body was taken from under the rubble of my grandmother's house... when I woke up, I was unexpectedly surrounded by the whiteness of the hospitals' bloodstained walls... someone was rinsing the flooded-with-blood floor, red was the stream that spilled in to the drain at the doorstep! I smelled my uncle then. I could not imagine that the blood I saw was his. I was not delusional when I saw my uncle turning into a thread of blood flowing in a small river to mix with the soil of the back street of the hospital!

For a few moments, I was crying in a hysteric way. My body spasm and I fell into a coma. But I did not know how long it lasted.

For years, my uncle's body was getting up in my dream from the rubble, gathering its pieces and laughing in rage. My uncle was tough. He had a strong tone and personality, however when we saw him, his smile used to make us forget the mixed with fears dread. Out of kindness, my uncle used to drive us to my grandfather's land in the mountain, grill some soft meat for us to eat and let us climb the trees and rocks, watching us while he was drinking tea, and yell saying:

"Do not go so far, be careful, the rocks are high and there are snakes' dens."

I used to imagine my uncle as a part of this great mountain. He would remain as long as the rocks, old trees, and soil. Deep down inside, I denied his death until once I saw a video on YouTube that showed his land empty from the olive trees, and the trees of walnuts and cherry were turned into ashes in the stoves of this poor city.

I cried that day until the hot air of Antakya's mountain dried my tears and heart.

On the top there, where Niel and I one day watched the rays of the sun descending towards sunset, I fell asleep on my sadness and loneliness... and saw him getting closer... the soldier, who once broke into our house a few hours before shelling, was holding something in his hands and mockingly laughing? "What do you think about this lingerie? I found it in the closet in your house."

No one in our house wears these things...

كنت أصرخ وصدى صوت موحش يطرق رأسي بقوة، لمست وعي بحين فتحت عيني لأيلم أعرف يسري، الظلام الميم من لهى للمكان أضاع ملامحه، تلمست جسدي، كل شيء في المكل متقرب.. نهضت ببطء وقبل أن تهدأ ضربات قلبي انطلعت في الطريق الترابي بسرعة غير مبالاة بالحجار والحصى والتراب المتطاير حولي...

(I was screaming, and the echo of a lonely voice is hammering my head strongly, I didn't recognize when I opened my eyes that I wasn't in my bed, The darkness that prevailed over the place made it lose its features, I touched my body, everything was almost in place... I stood up slowly and before my heartbeat calmed, I rushed down the narrow soil road at a speed, unfazed by stones, pebbles and dirt flying around me...).

The wild monstrous music of the universe was pouring in my ears, harsh and loud on a quite hot night, as if I were rolling inside of copper vessels crashing into the rocks hidden in the dark... sarcastic laughs stumbling my steps, I turned, nobody around!

From far, I saw the slightly lightened cement road. When I stepped on the sidewalk, I felt a kind of violent dizziness that knocked me down. I called Marie, "please come fast."

I felt a hand patting my hair, his tender voice came to me clear and calm… "Do not care, baby, I will pray for you next time to take the top mark in exam."

My grandfather's hand was both warm and kind. It made me feel safe and gave me great doses of confidence. I felt I would be alright because of his prayers. Before he died, I was sure when I did not take the full mark in exam that he forgot to pray for me while praying. I lifted my head slowly; for a few seconds I thought the smiley encouraging face was his.

"Give me your hand."

I gave him my hands and we got up… it was not too long till we arrived at the Meclis Café. I had coffee while I was feeling blue. Marie asked gently:

"What happened? Why did you climb the mountain alone? I will not ask you about fear, I want to know the reason."

I said with bitterness in my throat:

"My uncle died."

And I cried wildly. Marie waited until I went quiet and asked:

"Do you have a third one that I do not know? How did he

die? Or do you mean your uncle from your father's family?"

"No, my uncle from my mom's. Today I saw his land with no trees."

Marie said with confidence:

"But rocks and soil are still there. You did not link his existence only to the trees, trees are human made. He planted them and they grew, and he lived from their fruits, but soil is there from the beginning of time and also the rocks, or do you have other thoughts on that?"

"You know I have not accepted the idea of death since my grandfather died. Older family members are a necessity in my life, they gave me not only a sense of intimacy but also confidence. After losing the people whom we love, the world became empty and barren. You know I could not prevent her from going. Much worse, I could not go with her, either. She insists on dying back home. She does not want to die in a strange country; she wants to be beside her kids, mother and husband… I do not know exactly how to explain to you, even I cannot understand my contradictory and conflicting feelings about one same thing. All I know is that I blame her a lot in my heart for that she has been the last hope I have. I felt as if she pulled my soul from my body and took it with her… why do those whom we love insist on killing us in the name of love?"

When my grandfather died, I could not understand the secret behind his absence. I was too young, and I could not find the warm hand that used to pat my hair and give me internal as well as external security. How could a hand touch change one's fate? That is what happened; my life changed when I lost the touch of his hand on my hair.

I could not imagine what happened, it was so hard to me

to accept someone's death even in the normal way. I faced the news with an utter cowardice like other pieces of news. Every time, I convinced myself that who was gone was still here, and I could see them whenever I wanted… I used to sneak into my grandpa's room, turn off the lights and blame him for abandoning me… once I heard his voice telling me that he did not, and would never leave me alone, and that he would bring me the candy I love… that night I slept deeply. I waited for the sweets he promised, and when I woke up in the morning, I found the sweets bag near to my bed… what surprised me was that he did not just bring me candy but also sometimes used to leave me notes written on them with a very good handwriting: "I love you sweetheart".

The surprise was when I grew up and went to high school, I discovered that the handwriting was never my grandfather's, and that deep voice that one day came out of the darkness was my uncle's. It was a coincidence he was laying in my grandpa's bed and heard me blaming him for leaving me, so he replied! Until now I refuse to believe they are gone, my grandpa, my uncle, my aunt and my brother… I refuse to think that they are not on earth anymore, I won't be able to smell them anymore, won't hear their voices, no one will reproach me for not doing something in the right way… none…

They wouldn't come back, they were never even here someday… if I believed the idea that they had been gone, I should convince myself that they were here once… they turned into an idea my mind could not possibly handle to be true.

For years I felt my brain was like an old computer that stopped working as if I had opened a hundred pages together. I denied in all ways possible their deaths, and my mind kept convincing me that they were still alive… they are, someplace.

My uncle is in the mountain, whereas my grandpa is in the eastern land. My aunt is visiting her mom-in-law, while my brother is studying in Damascus and will be back soon. To my great astonishment, this kind of belief gave me strength and certainty that everything is alright, but soon it reflected on my study and my relationship with my friends. I started to fall back significantly until I became completely marginalized and hated going to school, and I turned away from my girlfriends and started to feel that they were much better and more successful than I was.

I could not defeat that feeling easily, and others were not convinced by my reasons. That was why they used to gossip and whisper (lucky the one you are thinking about). I never cared for one day about their thoughts!

My grandma was the only one connected to my pain. She tried to relieve me from my sufferings because it was the same suffering that she was also going through. She also had her own annoying depression bouts that she used to defeat with all the faith she had and trusted in God.

I am a human being who can find salvation in dreams. My imagination, dreams and intuition are the main components in my personality, for my intuition and my night dreams push me towards decisions I am convinced were estimated for me and written in the Book of Life and that I cannot resist it or change… sometimes it occurs to me that the reason it happens is my deep faith, that it might be an occult power dominating the way my day goes. What happened in 2011 was never out of context for me. Deep inside, there was something about to explode and make me fly high. That thing was mixed with fear and a lump in my throat. It slaughtered me in the early morning and left me suffering depression, permeated by waves of joy, as if I had taken a hallucinatory drug.

Not a month passed on that feeling till the demonstrations exploded around the country demanding freedom.

So, it is "freedom" that makes wings to the body and programs the mind to refuse to submit to the domination of individualism and the existing system.

***

In April 2018, they informed us that the organization was going to shut. It was a shocking piece of news to me despite all the previous indications that warned us that it wouldn't continue and that we had to think seriously about finding another job. That happened after they found out about the fraud Abo Ahmad did, the one who is responsible for the office inside Syria, who stole most of the aids for almost four years of working with the organization. It was not the only thing he did, but also, he used to distribute aid and food baskets for families that were not in need just to gain the Al-Nusra Front's silence on his behalf. The aids used to go to Al-Nusra Front's families and to Abo Ahmad's bucket. The mere fact that he helped Al-Nusra Front is illegal to the organization's rules. Abu Abdo thus closed the doors of aids in the face of the poor people inside, and in the face of all the employees of the organization outside and inside Syria.

In waves we left the work, after closing the files and giving them to the donors, and I was with the August wave. In the middle of the hot August, I found myself depressed and unemployed, and felt like the gates of hell had opened with the increase of temperature and lethal humidity and the spread of mosquitoes because of the drought of Asi. Then, I decided to search for work in other cities. Gaziantep was the closest and the most crowded with Arab and Syrians especially, and work there was available, but I did not love that city! I do not know the reason why I dislike it, though it is the closest Turkish city to Syria and looks like Aleppo. It has a similar atmosphere, the lanes, the arcades, and some of the people's traditions. Maybe this similarity is the reason I refused the city that makes me live in the past, as if time stopped since the very second the car passed the camels convoy status that refers to the silk road.

Days passed slowly and bleakly because I could not find a job, and what was left from my salary could be barely enough for a few months. I had to take an important decision in a few days, especially after I left alone.

My relatives who were living with me left the house in Turkey for Europe in the boats of death, searching for better living circumstances after they had suffered for years from working in restaurants, ovens, and other kinds of jobs which were considered to be a humiliation for someone who was forced to get out of his home land searching for his freedom and dignity.

Antakya now was detestably desolate. I wondered if I was going to hate the lovely city with its streets, atmosphere, and life details. However, when I went out to the cold streets in winter while wearing my red coat, it brought me back the memories of siege back in my city. It was a very cold winter with a very expensive fuel. The city was almost out of it; nevertheless, my grandma bought enough to light during the winter nights. Besides, we put a very big barrel under the gutter to collect the rain water, so we could boil it and take a shower. We sat the whole evening on kerosene bulb light, and we knitted wool, and I used sometimes to study books and plays assigned to us in university. One of them was 'Doctor Faustus'. How I wished to do what he had done, sold my soul to the devil and got a better life for me and my grandma. As well I could have a friend to entertain me like Mephistophilis, even if he was temporary.

Despite the very cold weather then, I could not wear heavy clothes; they suffocated me. I used to wear a long red coat and walk on the freezing ground in the university with high heel red shoes. My colleagues used to call me "the lady in red" and my heart was a piece of flame like Howel's heart from 'Howel's Moving Castle'.

The dreariest history started when my parents decided to go to Europe, enterprising with sending my little brother first so he could get a residency and apply for family reunification.

I was above eighteen when they traveled, and they could no longer pull me there. Finally I understood the meaning of the folk saying, "someone is cut from a tree!"

I was about to cut all my relationships with Antakya when an Italian journalist friend Shwan called and said that he was coming with a Swedish journalist and that she wanted my help as a translator for her and the refugees that she was going to do research about. Because I was alone, Shawn suggested my having Ida as a guest at my place during her stay in Antakya.

Ida came from the Scandinavian cold cities, and she looked like Disney princesses. She had a unique kind of beauty near to the mermaids in magazines, thanks to her blond hair, blue eyes, and her height.

I took her to Arsuz after she told me about her desire to swim after a long week of work.

I told her: "I cannot swim." She said: "I can teach you." She used to teach kids to swim in Sweden. Ida had a tattoo on her back in Arabic, which she had done in Lebanon. It said: "We do what is done by the unemployed and prisoners… we raise hope", and she did teach me how to swim, first like a frog, and then to dive; it was difficult for me at the beginning, but when I started to dive, I wished I could stay under water. If I were a fish and ended up in a shark stomach or some fisherman's bucket, at least I would not tire myself in imagining the way I would die. What I really feared the most was drowning to death in the sea in some boat going to Europe. Maybe for that reason, I did not dare to travel to my parents.

We used to sit in my room's balcony with a fruit plate and smoke cigarettes. We talked about everything in our lives, we shared so much information, and we discovered so many mutual things. Ida turned to me one evening and said:

- "You look familiar, like someone I knew from my childhood. Rarely do I feel comfortable with strangers the way I feel with you, like sisters."

This was exactly what I felt. We both were like sisters grown up in different countries, or maybe she was my best friend in my previous life. Considering my bad luck in most things, it was not the case in getting good friends. I always had good friends, feeling like they were from a parallel universe. I felt over the moon for getting Ida as a new friend, or even a sister.

Once again, after she left, I felt big emptiness inside my heart, for she was so real to an imaginary level!

***

Craving Reeds.
I used to hear its voice coming from the closet where the wool

doll that my grandma knitted in my childhood was. That dim nostalgia in the voice drove me to cry and it clenched my neck with fingers of thorns...

At the beginning, I thought locking the doll in the closet under the clothes would prevent its voice from coming to me, but what happened was that the voice was not low. The first night the doll slept in the closet, it was suffocated and choppy, but clear, sneaking with confidence and pressing my throat, so I burst into tears.

It was not easy to me to give up the doll in throwing it or giving it to some kid... I brought it with me during my displacement trip after hesitation and I put it on a small table near to my bed. More surprisingly, my doll since we had displaced went mute. I could no longer hear the calamitous sound of a flute on the banks of the river where we once lived... the river never left us, and we never forgot it. Maybe that was why Asi river was one of the reasons that linked me to Antakya, though of its draught and bad smell it constantly blew it. The geographical similarity had a great effect on me choosing the city, though in the beginning it was merely a coincidence...

Today, surprisingly, I woke up on that sound, but it was far away from a flute sound; it was more like the voice of a bereaved mother amid destruction that never left my soul... I put my fingers in my ears, but the sound got louder along with the increasing of my heart beats...was that because I saw a nightmare that shook me strongly? No doubt, it was a nightmare effect, there was no way what was happening to me was true. In spite of my beliefs, the sound did not vanish; it kept knocking in my ears, leaving tinnitus, disturbing my heartbeats.

Something involuntary made me hold it and run, searching for scissors. I do not know how my heart obeyed me, and my hands helped me tear and scatter the wool in pieces in the room corners until the flute fell on the ground, slightly moaned, and the universe went silence around me.

It is the story! My grandma's story. Tears filled my eyes. I was five years old when my grandmother knitted the doll for me. She told me that she put something so precious of heart inside of it that her father gifted her when she was a child. My grandma had a beautiful voice. She had loved music and singing since she was a little kid, and her father brought her a flute that he made himself and taught her how to play on it. After he died, my grandma stopped singing in front of other people and kept the flute inside a closed box.

My grandmother! The flute! She gave me her most valuable assets. The purest melodies the flute kept with her breaths and soul...

Everything went silent, my doll died, and I could no longer fix it. The flute as well went silent and left the mission of planting fear in my heart to darkness with weird voices coming from inside the apartment, though I already locked the windows and the doors.

I curled up on myself in bed, long hours passed, morn got closer, and I could not fall asleep... everything around me terrified me.

When daylight started seeping through the window, a small nap took me home. I saw myself going up the stairs of our house, and I heard clearly the voice of my grandfather calling out my grandmother to bring him a warm water bucket to prepare to pray... I heard my uncle's voice and saw him peeping at me from the small room, asking with blame: "why didn't you come back to visit me? You were too late; did you not promise me a visit every Friday?" Did I promise my uncle?

I wanted to say, "here I came", but my voice failed me. I could not speak. I walked to the sitting room. My aunt, as always, was watching a Turkish series and wiping her tears that always fell unwillingly. I sat on a chair near the door and asked her, "did Yahia and Lamis get married, my aunt? Why did such things make you cry since you knew it was just acting?" But again, my voice failed me.

I wanted to ask about my grandma, but my voice got stuck in my throat... I got up to look for her in the kitchen... the hot rice pudding was lined on the kitchen ceramic slab elegantly, smelling of cinnamon and orange blossom water... I whispered, "Grandma". I did not hear my voice and I did not see my grandma.

My grandpa called again, "bring the rice pudding for me and for..." It was mine and my grandpa's favorite meal, that my grandma made especially for us.

"Dalal..." once again, my grandpa called, but I did not hear my grandma answering... I held the door's handle and wanted to open it. It opened by itself, it opened on a burning room, and in the middle of it was the soldier who broke into our house holding the remains of a dead child. Her body was without a head but in a weird way I felt she was Farah's daughter!

I woke up terrified with one idea controlling my mind... "My grandmother died!"

The news of Marie's sudden illness and emaciation was bad and shocking. My heart hurt. Since I knew Ida, I wondered, "is there anyone else going to disappear from my life?"

Oddly, I was relieved that the doctors could not determine the type of what she was suffering from despite the tests, the x-rays, and the MRI scan that the doctor recently requested.

With an empty mind I was going to clinics, waiting with her, helping her change her clothes, carry her bag. In doing so, I felt satisfied whenever they asked her to do a new test. With that, I got rid of the concept of a disease that worried me. I thanked God and smiled as if I were possessed... even Marie started looking at me wondering what had been wrong with me!

I told her maybe it was the delusional disease, or love, and that she was not suffering from a physiological disease and should stop paying stupid doctors her money. Nevertheless, she did not think the same. She told me her pain had been real and that her body often let her down, and she fell unconscious in the street.

For four months, Maraym lost much weight and she moved like a ghost, needing someone to lay on while walking. More surprisingly, Marie asked me, while waiting for the test results she did for the thyroid, "is there any news about Niel?"

Words refused to come out. Hurting, I said, "I'm still waiting for his call. I am sure he is in love with me, but maybe he needs some time, maybe because of the age difference, and perhaps the environmental and cultural differences, perhaps... I do not know exactly, but I find all of these reasons dumb, and they have no meaning. They are no more than excuses."

"Why do you not call? What are you waiting for?"

Being emotionally touched, I did not need her to repeat the request. I was waiting for someone to take responsibility for the feeling that I was acting foolishly. I called him!

His tone was tough and cruel, as if he were writing a daily

report to his work. With the same apathy, Niel left his cup of coffee to get cold, and then he threw it in the sink to make another hot one. He waited until the last flame thread faded from the mug's surface, sipped a little, with irritated features, pushed the cup to the far end of the table and continued his work… that weird habit was not arbitrary; it was an accurate expression of Niel's temper and his distrust of things around him…

We talked before about faith, religion, and other aspects of life, yet I knew that he had not believed in metaphysical things except the things he touched with his own fingers and saw in his eyes. More particularly, seeing was believing for Niel, not the other way around. His weird way of thinking and temperaments never held me back from falling in love with him. When a female is in love, she never sees the truth. The complete blindness situation was over while we were talking on the phone. I found myself facing someone no one could love but a naive girl like me.

Marie took my shivering body in her skinny hands. I was shivering vigorously and sobbing with a loud voice that attracted the attention of all those in the cafe. Even the waiter intervened with a cup of lemon I did not order with a cup of cold water.

Mariae said calmly, "Wipe your tears. I knew everything, and I wanted you to know. Niel never was yours and he did not love you, he could not be connected to a place like you, and he never liked romantic love stories and could not understand the feeling of an eastern woman. He just wanted to spend time. You were right in front of him, in love with him and available. He is just a big coward telling you he could not come to Antakya for security reasons! How easy is it for him to lie?

But is he lying for a teenager, thinking that you are going to believe him? He says that he is getting drunk and cannot leave the house or wake up? Believe me when I say, he will find another woman the next day. I know these kinds of people through my work in organizations. I have to shock you, so you can get rid of the illusion controlling you. You have to know; he is the biggest loser here. Each shock will make us stronger, and those traumas will make you stronger and more able to understand others. It is true that the stronger the wind, the stronger the trees.

"Is it really? Is he the loser or me? I feel disappointed and oppressed, for that I have been stupid for a year of waiting, during which I built dreams that reached heaven. I saw myself living with him in the US, continuing my study, building a new life, but he destroyed everything so easily."

"You built, he did not. He did not build his dreams with you; he was thinking separately and lived separately as if you did not exist. To be honest, he was not responsible for your lack of knowledge in his personality."

"I am the responsible idiot!"

"No, it is love that covers defects, blinds the sight and leaves all the senses in chaos, so feelings get confused and clashed, and there is no room left for you to see clearly. Do not blame yourself a lot, you will get rid of all these things soon and you will say, 'Marie said so'."

I smiled amid my tears:

"Nothing to say after what Marie has said… I know."

I decided to leave Antakya to live in Istanbul, a final decision. I could no longer look at the mountain that once witnessed my love, from the windows, streets, everywhere I go.

The house I rented in Istanbul did not fit the size of my dream. It was for an old lady who died a short while ago and her daughter rented out the apartment furnished. It had a bedroom, sitting room, a kitchen and a small bathroom. It works in a big loud city, for that who lives there does not need but walls where he can fulfill his needs of sleeping, eating, and bathing, and spend the rest of his time out...

The city has a great deal of temptation that a visitor cannot resist, and if it had not been super expensive, it would have been one of the best cities for permanent residence.

In the grandmother's house, there was an old Singer sewing machine. Rumors say the machine needle contains red mercury, which is alleged to be used in the nuclear weapons industry, and for that, some websites estimated the price of the machine for fifty thousand dollars.

For me, the sewing machine was a talisman for protection from black magic, which I once believed in, and it was remarkably similar to my grandmother's sewing machine that used to make me summer dresses and amazed me with its beauty and mastery. When I was a child, I used to sit on the ground beside my grandma while she sewed clothes and collected scraps of the fabric that she threw on the floor to make clothes for my doll out of. She taught me once how to sew pants...

She was proud of me that day and loved my accomplishment. She showed it to her visitors and praised me for how fast I learned the craft and told them that I would one day be a great fashion designer in addition to my proficiency in drawing.

I often feel guilty that I disappointed my grandmother; I did not become a great painter as she predicted and did not study fashion design as she hoped... sometimes, colors surround me and force me to drawing for days with paper. More perplexingly, when I finish, I feel a great emptiness and dissatisfaction with the painting that I have finished. Every painting carries with it a sense of disappointment. Besides, with every painting, I feel that I do not make any progress and that my paintings are not good enough to show them to others. That frustrating feeling makes my fingers crusty, so I feel as if they were just wood cut off from their trees and were no longer suitable for life.

Fear accompanied me in the new home, so I started running away from it to cafes, and visiting touristic places, but was forced to go back at night and bury my body in bed, trying to sleep faster. However, obsessions start to ravage my heart and imagination, and made me think that there was movement in the house. At the very beginning, I thought the grandma who owned the house came back every night to check on her stuff. I was so sure until one day, while I was about to sleep, and heard the sound of the Singer machine. It was not a dream for sure. I opened my eyes, feeling shocked by the guy standing in the next building at the window. He smiled at me and waved his hand as if he were inviting me to talk. I hung the curtain nervously and went back to bed. Actually, I did not dare to leave the bedroom and go through the sitting room... I was dreadfully scared, as the sound of the Singer machine became louder, accompanied by the sound of the rustle of the cloth, until I almost recognized its type!

A very loud laugh reached my ears, and several laughs came after the first one. The sound of cups knocked against each other and hustle I did not know before... the next room to the bedroom which was separated from the same house inhabited by guys. It was the habit of the guys to stay up late at night and get drunk; their voices got louder and louder, day in and day out. I heard the sound of their steps as if they were passing through the wall, coming to me!

To overcome my annoying sleeping difficulties, I started to take sleeping pills in order to keep my nerves from collapsing. On the first day, I slept deeply and in the morning my head was heavy as if I were holding a rock on my shoulders… I drunk a whole pot of coffee and went out of the house. Next day, I was worried somehow. On the third day, I woke several times due to my painfully strong heart beats, as if I was waking up to a strong explosion, or something heavy falling to the ground of the living room, the roof maybe!

The fourth day, I was awakened by the frogs' croaking sound… the lovely sound that I used to hear in Antakya coming from Asi river, with burgos and mosquito bites… I noticed a painful itch in my fingers caused by a fresh sting!

On the fifth day, the sleeping pills no longer affected me. I felt terrified and my heart beats were getting stronger… and the usual nightmare invaded my sleep and prevented me from sleeping ...

The last time I felt such exhaustion and fatigue was in Syria; more specifically, in the summer of 2012, when my city was besieged by the regime forces for almost a month. During this month, there was no electricity, and because of that, we could not store any food in the refrigerator. Moreover, we could not buy any vegetables, only from the passing cars. Therefore, most of the times we bought zucchini to my uncle's wife to fry it and to dip in yogurt for lunch. In the whole building that my mom's family owns, there was only my grandma, my uncle's wife, her daughter, my uncle's eldest son's wife with her two kids, and me there. We used to spend our time in the kitchen or the corridor until evening came and the shelling stopped. Each morning, we woke up on the sound of drones that often broke the sound wall. My cousin kept reading the Holy Qur'an while I laid down on the corridor floor carelessly to take the coldness stored in it and read the myths of love: echoes of Greek and Roman mythology. My habit hasn't changed much from that time, I guess. I ignore my fear till it floats to the surface, causing me so many problems later. After siege, the inspection began, and it was the most terrifying part of all, for we were only women in a five-floor building without any protection. Out of fear, my uncle's wife welcomed the soldiers warmly and offered them hot tea, and after they had finished, they searched the building houses one after another. The last one was my grandmother's house where we gathered all. My cousin's kids were asleep, and they woke them up. More badly, one soldier held Ossama between his hands and asked: "where is your father?" Ossama answered: "he is with the free army, wearing just like you and holding a rifle." At that time, I felt the poison spreading through my body from the tips of my toes to my head. I felt a slight sense of dizziness, but I couldn't move so I stood still. My grandma who was sitting on the chair beside the door, she was fearfully fixed in her place and her pupils dilated, and it seemed to me that force rushed into her hands until I felt that the wooden chair arms that she was holding were about to crush. The soldier asked: "what is the father's name?" My grandma answered quickly, "Anas, he was serving in the army, a soldier in Deir ez-Zur." On that day, we miraculously survived. When they went out, I felt as though I did not possess my body and that my head was about to fall as if it had been cut off very quickly.

The soldier comes in a different shape every time, and in every dream, he carries a strange weapon ... He throws me to the ground and cuts my neck ... I get up washed with sweat, I shiver strongly ... his face does not change, it is that soldier who broke into our house! After soldiers had searched the house and left, he came back alone a few minutes later, he locked the door to the room where my grandmother was sitting and dragged me to the small side room...

He still holds the headless body of Farah's daughter.

***

I hated nothing in Turkey as much as I hated the Turkish language. I could not, and I would not want to learn. What helped me with that was the fact that I worked with foreigners who used English, and because most of Antakya's inhabitants speak Arabic, but it is different in Istanbul where I was living now, and I did not know the language of its people, and they do not speak English even in restaurants and airports... Turks are very committed to their language, and they address visitors as if it was their duty to know Turkish, otherwise why are they here?!

Three months had passed since I came to Istanbul. Three months and I could not find a job and lived from my savings from my previous job. I do not know what made me sign myself up for Spanish classes in Cervantes instead of learning Turkish, the language of the country I lived in. Was it yearning that kept dragging me to Niel's swamp where frogs resided and transformed at night into lovers who celebrate their wedding in the light of the stars scattered in the nearby sky!

Niel, I think he is the reason, he who is pushing me to

learn Spanish that he fluently speaks. He is the one who still surrounds my soul with an energy from fire of passion, longing, and yearning. When will I get rid of the traces of his devastating love?

Three months passed. I could only sleep for a few hours when the sun started to rise into the afternoon. I was afraid constantly. More dangerous, frightening nightmares never left me for the whole time. When I started to fall asleep in the morning, it seemed to me that the seagulls' sound was just a sarcastic laugh mocking me and my failure which I do not really consider a failure now. I woke up intermittently after every nightmare fixed in fear, as if a thousand needles had been injected all over my body. More unexpectedly, I felt the sweat that had started coming out of my scalp, and the cold was almost freezing the tips of my fingers. The sounds in my head never stopped until I started imagining that there was someone staring in the corner of the room, watching me while asleep until the time came, and he pounced on me. I could not stop thinking about suicide, one of the worst nightmares I suffered from in February.

My grandmother's death...
It was so hard for me for one second that at some time my grandma would die. Over the years my mind convinced me that my grandmother was immortal, which would make it harder for me to accept her death, and maybe I felt that way because she was really tough. For me, she was the strongest woman I had ever seen, she was my role model. More interestingly, in her youth my grandmother learned sewing by her own, so she wouldn't be in need for money from anyone, especially if he was a man. She raised seven kids and dressed

them from what she sewed. Out of love, she did the same with her grandsons through summers and winters. Psychologically speaking, I got used to her healing hands braiding my hair right before I went to school, and her helping me with my math homework that I never understood then, until I grew up and started combing her hair. I felt an exaggerated kind of happiness when she asked me to comb and tie her hair as if I was touching a holy thing that I should not have touched.

One morning, I almost made a foolish act by throwing the Singer machine into the street as I did with my doll... but the machine was not mine. Actually, I had no right to do anything with it.

I hate horror movies so much, and I cannot for once watch one without so many people telling me "the nightmares you see are caused by your addiction to horror movies". No one can imagine that the reality I have lived is more violent than those films... no, no one who has not lived the circumstances that I lived can ever imagine what really happened!

The harassment I went through from Turkish guys while I was returning home in Mecidiyekoy after eleven at night, and the defense from the black guys living in the neighborhood for me, made me think in a serious way to learn boxing. For this reason, I asked my friend about a place where I could train. Gladly, they told me about a gym owned by a young Syrian guy migrated from Homs after he was injured in the battles that happened in Baba Amr.

"The pain you feel now will become a strength." This was written on the wall of the gym and that was really what gave me a real motivation. Every time I read the sentence, I got more attached to the pain that was probably going to make a strong person out of me. This was what I started to feel after time had passed, until I began to regain the confidence that I had lost for so long and which had been destroyed by a number of ignorant people.

I started my training for two days a week, and it started to increase with the increasing of my strength. I woke up early every training day and drank a small cup of coffee with exactly two dried pieces of apricot. After that, I wore my clothes and went out at ten fifteen... from my house to the main street, it was full of shops in addition to some clothes and shoes stalls. Before I arrived in the main street, there were those who played the stolen phones in wooden boxes that have small glass doors. Every time I saw them, I remembered the same boxes, but full of delicious pieces of cake decorated with small pieces of jelly on the top, put in front of each market in my home town when I was five to six years old. Some days I bought nothing at school and would be content with the thyme sandwich that my mother put in my bag before I went out with the apple, so I could buy the cake when I came out of school. On some other days I just could not resist the smell of fresh sweet bread that the seller had just finished baking and took out the oven, or even the pink and yellow sugar sticks. Once, my cousin and I missed the school march. We went from a side street and bought colored ice cream and stayed there until the end of the march so that the teacher would not see us. Unfortunately, ice cream and cake will never have the same taste that it used to when I was a kid. I wish life had stopped in that side street, because I was so happy, and I couldn't have those moments of happiness even in my daydreams.

I crossed the street so I could take the Şişli – Taksim metro on my way after I had got out the metro in Taksim close to Ali Sports Club. There was a mini market. I went in to buy one banana to boost my activity during training and a liter of water to drink half of during training, and to finish one hour after the training ended at twelve o'clock, maybe.

Ali was neither tall neither short. He was a young man with medium muscles, but he had extraordinary power in his body and mind. Pleasurably, we had more than one conversation during training, and we became friends in a short period of time. During that time, he invited me to have a cup of coffee with his wife. His wife was a young, educated, elegant and beautiful Lebanese woman. She was very friendly the whole evening we spent together, and I was surprised that she was a psychiatrist when she made some notes about my personality, and she offered to help me in case I felt the need to talk about myself and my problems.

I do not deny that I was very comfortable with her, and it occurred to me that I would visit her in the clinic more than once, but I hesitated. Honestly speaking, I was afraid to confront myself by talking about it in front of others, and I did not like others to know about me something other than what I offered them with my full will and desire.

"The egg from which the soldiers come out."
"What are you most afraid of?"

That was the first question she asked me when I visited her clinic for the first time. I didn't want to undergo the experience of seeing a psychiatrist, but Lia, who invited me to have a cup of coffee, made special influence on me when she asked me about the kind of music I like. I said:

"Swan Lake."

She put the cylinder in an old phonograph, dimmed the lights, and shared the cup of coffee with me quietly. She suddenly said:

"Why do you not make yourself comfortable? Take off the shoes, high-heeled shoes, somehow just to depressurize the nerves."

I took off the shoes and took a deep breath...

"I think you want to relax on the sofa."

I got up from the chair, laid down on the sofa, and closed my eyes for a few seconds.

I heard Lia's voice asking me what I had feared most, and my answer surprised me: "The soldiers who came out of the egg."

I imagined the reaction on Lia's face, asking me:

"How did soldiers get out of the egg?"

I smiled:

"These orange soldiers, don't you know them? They are not always orange, sometimes they are green."

"Do you call the chicks that come out of eggs 'soldiers'? Where is the similarity between them and the soldiers?"

I enjoyed the game; Lia still did not get what I meant:

"No, but the soldiers who entered our house, they wore camouflage clothes. Among them, there was only one soldier wearing black clothes, and folding his forehead was a green ribbon, he was neither orange nor green anyway... they rushed out of the tanks just as the orange soldiers pushed out from inside the egg. The difference is that the weapons of those who raided our house - they used the name of the raid squadron - are real and blood will flow when they use them... as for the orange soldiers, they were peaceful and only mastered the language of silence and surrender when we threw them on the ground and trampled them with our little feet, however, they terrified me, and I did not like them... the problem was that I had soldiers from the egg, including a black one... my brothers refused to exchange me for their cute toys, including ships and cars."

"I see... it is then related to a childhood fear of toys hidden inside chocolate eggs. Do you hate chocolate?"

"I love it very much, but I do not like the egg-shaped ones or the ones that hide coconut or liquid caramel inside. I do not like surprises of this kind. I always have disturbing memories that end with illness and sometimes death. This happened to a friend of mine in my childhood after she ate chocolate with spoiled liquid."

Lia asked me:

"How do you see yourself? Tell me about you?"

I was not the person who could show any reaction to any problem or trauma that occurred directly, rather, I would bury them in the darkness of my depths and forget them until they floated to the surface causing tremendous destruction. Furthermore, I am not good at dealing with people. This is what made them turn away from me after knowing me for a short time. More precariously, the people I became a friend with saw me with their souls rather than with their eyes. I always felt strange to the people I met, as if I were from another planet. Deep within, I felt sad every time someone got away, only because I was not like them. Sometimes, I felt deficient until I discovered that I was not lacking anything. The problem facing people was that I was open and receptive to others, but they were fanatical about their ideas and their way of living. I remembered that when I started working in the second organization in Antakya, my colleagues used to say I was a weirdo in English. I always understood it in a negative sense, but it was a positive thing all the time, for it was my strangeness that differentiated me from others!

I never went back again to Lia's clinic. A friend called and told me that there was a job opportunity if I wanted to apply. I did not have another choice, a job in Gaziantep might be better than waiting for nothing in Istanbul… with that, I was preparing myself to visit her again to tell her the details about the story of the raiding soldier who broke into our house and turned my life into hell and killed Farah's daughter.

***

The last thing I expected was to meet Kabir khan at Sabiha Gokcen Airport hall after five years since the organization where we worked together closed in Antakya.

I was in front of the electric board looking at my trip number and which gate it was, when I felt a hand touching my shoulder. I shivered and turned around to face Kabir khan with his gloomy face and his pale skin. Astonishingly, Kabir khan was a different person as the last five years of absence left bad effects on his features and made him look a little bit older than he was. In particular, his thick black hair was ruthlessly conquered by white hair, a young man at the end of his third decade who looked fifty years old. At that moment, I did not know what to say. He started talking:

"Can I invite you to have a cup of coffee before your trip time comes?"

"Why not."

I hardly said the word. I did not know why I agreed, maybe it was my curiosity to know what happened with him after this time, and maybe because I needed to spend some time after my trip was delayed because of the bad weather.

Chapter II

Antakya 2014
Snow Departure

Kabir khan was my manager. In the beginning, it was hard for me to understand him because of his weird accent. When he spelled English words, I had difficulty communicating with him. Therefore, I used to nod my head affirmatively on a talk I did not understand half of. He was in his thirties; he was tall with a skinny body to a point that made him look sick. His skin was brown, and his eyes were sunken into two large pits that gave them a sense of sadness. Rarely did he smile and laugh. Morally speaking, Kabir khan was so polite, but quick to anger. When he was angry, words flew out of his mouth with a surprising speed that prevented me from comprehending what he was saying. Yet, I felt he cursed and scolded, and when he calmed down, he ordered a cup of tea and issued brief commands that summarized what he had said during anger.

Kabir khan was handsome, but he was not liked by the workers in the organization regardless of their different nationalities. I do not know what made me respond to his sudden courtship.

We were together one day after working hours when he asked me to re-classify some information while everyone else was gone. All of a sudden, I felt overwhelmed, and I wanted to object, but something serious and stern in his eyes made me go back to the office. I opened my computer and re-classified as he asked me to do.

I did not notice the time while he was talking to me about complex things that were not closely related to the work. After I had finished, he said simply:

"You are late, can I walk you home?"

I did not find his offer bad, for I was living far from downtown in a place called Toki, which were several modern buildings, followed by agricultural lands connected to the mountains. Only dog sounds could be heard at night and chickens in the morning. The habitants were a mix of Turks and refugees. Amidst the buildings, there were spaces designed for playing objects for kids and seats for elderly people, frequented by a few elderly women and a few children.

When we got to the area, it was past nine in the evening. During this time, the movement was less until I arrived at the building. Scarcely did I meet a human being walking the long street. For we were living in the last road that the bus did not reach. Kabir khan insisted to accompany me to the door of the building, then to the door of the apartment to make sure I was safe.

He hemmed as I opened the door and said in funny Arabic, "O people of the house." My grandma answered from inside:

"Come in."

Kabir khan did not wait after she had invited him. He entered the living room and told her:

"Now that she is safe, excuse me."

My grandma said:

"Come in, drink some coffee."

He answered with confidence:

"I will leave it to another time, let it be an invitation for dinner."

My grandma smiled and said:

"Welcome in any weekend, it is an honor, you are welcome."

The simplicity with which my grandmother and Kabir khan got to know each other did not leave a good impression on me. I did not want it to turn into a friendship or personal acquaintance between us, because I knew of Kabir khan's sharp and annoying character. More frankly, he was not good at laughing, and the smile did not know its way to his lips except by accident.

On Sunday, my grandma prepared all meals that she expected Kabir khan to like. He came on time; we sat down holding roses! For sure it was a miracle to see Kabir khan holding flowers, for it did not match his prickly nature, or at least that was what I imagined.

He did not stop talking about the city he came from, the people there, nostalgia, and how good his mom and sister-in-law were at cooking the whole time he spent with us.

He mentioned his brother's wife accidentally, and then my grandmother inquired about it:

"Do you all live together? I mean, your habits are similar to ours concerning family ties."

"Exactly grandma, we are Muslims."

The word had a bad effect on me, because I did not want to hear it the way it was said, it was weird. Why did Kabir khan want to pass a piece of information like that to my grandma, though she did not ask about his religion but only about the habits in his country! He added as if he felt my tension:

"I mean that our habits are similar because we are close

with what we believe in. Indian Muslim families still retain some traditions that the East generally adheres to, although times have changed a lot due to the information boom and other reasons that hit the traditional structure of the family system in our country."

I asked hesitantly:

"I know you are Pakistani!"

"It is true, I am from Pakistan, but Indian originally. I was born in the conflict zone where my ancestors were born and took possession of its lands and goods. Some call it 'the cursed paradise.' I do not know if you have heard of the disputed Kashmir region between India and Pakistan. I imagine you have not heard of it."

Though he was right with what he said, I was upset from what he said. It looked like a deliberated humiliation; it was his habit that he always reminded others of the shallowness of their culture and their knowledge about what was happening in the world outside the borders of their countries despite the information revolution that did not leave hard information out of reach. For that reason, precisely I read about the conflict between India and Pakistan and was really surprised by the amount of information that I did not know. I did not imagine that Pakistan was such a modern country and a strong country that possesses nuclear weapons!

The pieces of information I got about the place where Kabir khan came from were really shocking. The super powers of the world we live in are controlling countries that have been distinguished throughout history by their cultural and intellectual progress and gave the West the keys to urban and intellectual progress. However, Pakistan has proven to be a strong country despite everything being hatched against it. No one could return it to the ages of ignorance and keep it in the swamp of backwardness. India, too, I knew it from tales. I heard about the beauty of its architecture, its history, and its spices! I knew India looked like an Indian woman; I knew long ago one Indian woman who used to be a cleaning lady, from Ajara. A smile never left her face. To my satisfaction, she worked laughing, generous and lovely as much as she was neat and clean. I asked her once about her country's landmarks. She could not explain to me, but she said with her broken Arabic that her country was as usual very beautiful and hot, which made it special. I asked her if she knew the Taj Mahal. She said she had not visited it! Her answer struck me with frustration, as if I were the one who lived there and had not had the opportunity to see the dream "shrine", which I had always wished to visit because of what I heard about it.

Maybe I am like those who chase their dreams unconsciously, though I am linked to a small family who loves me. On the top of it, my grandma, who is keen not to get further dispersed and spread out more around the earth. That was what I told Kabir khan once during a conversation about traveling and working in Iraq in another organization with higher wages and would not be shut like what was happening in Turkey. The Turkish government was striving to close down every organization that did not adhere to the conditions it imposed on employing Turks and submit to Turkish control. Most of the time, an organization shut down the work it was doing because of these disagreements with the government. Our organization was about to close when Kabir khan talked about traveling and asked me if I wanted him to find me a job there.

For me, Iraq was not the country of dreams that I sought

to make true... I was searching for a scholarship in Europe, looking for a safer society, and working with organizations was nothing but a bridge on which I would cross to the dream. Everything in my life seemed temporary. Unluckily, I never felt settled where I had been or where I would be in a week, a month, or a year. I was sitting on a suitcase, and I might leave it too, for anywhere, and go empty-handed to buy another bag elsewhere in this world.

A few months after the organization had closed, we were preparing for it. Kabir khan invited me for a cup of coffee. I was not encouraged for accepting the invitation... for it came in the lost time as it occurred to me, but Kabir khan insisted on it. After work, I went to Meclis café in front of Atatürk status and Asi river... I found him waiting for me, although I arrived late. I did not apologize for even a small question as it should be. He said while trying to smile:

"I was about to leave."

"It is your name, do what you want if you want to leave now."

I unexpectedly got up.

He asked me in a faint voice to sit.

"You are too nervous today, aren't you?"

"Not more than you, I guess."

A semi-smile appeared on his lips:

"You are right, and maybe because of that I feel that we can easily understand each other, for I intended you with a favor to ask."

I was exceptionally nervous and motivated to attack, as if he had insulted me. He said after a few moments of silence:

"I want to get inside Syria, will you accompany me?"

I was so astonished that I did not ask him why and how.

All I thought about was those beautiful places I left behind years ago, Dad, Mom, my little brother, my aunts, and uncles… and a long list of my beloved ones who are now underground in the town cemetery, where to return? Can I really go back to that land, I whispered, as if I were enchanted?

"Where exactly do you want to go?"

"I need to meet some people in Sarmada, and then I will decide where. Now I do not know where exactly to go, but what I know now is that your presence with me will ease the border cross to me and your knowledge in the geography of the area will prevent others from deceiving me. Honestly, I am afraid of entering a place I know nothing about and do not speak its language. I need a translator I trust who never deceives me."

"The offer honestly does not suit me. I need to wear hijab and mantle to go with you, also I need to hide," said I.

"Do you not want to see your city?"

"I do not want to see destruction. My heart cannot handle it. Besides, my city is under regime control. I cannot enter it."

"Then, let us go to Saraqep. You have relatives there. Most importantly, they can help me with what I seek."

Then I noticed the important question I should have asked Kabir khan from the beginning; why he wanted to go to Syria. It was not work-related since the organization already had staff inside, and we do not need to monitor the work there. To my surprise, Kabir khan did not answer my question. Instead, he turned his face to the river side for minutes, retained rigid features, and then he turned to stare at me as if he were seeing me for the first time:

"Can I trust you? Do not misunderstand me, it is a little bit dangerous, and I did not tell anyone about it. I do not want you to take responsibility for actions you do not comprehend. To be honest, I want to search for my brother. More recently, I knew that he is in Ma'arat al-Nu'man and I understood that it is close to your city, but I do not trust the guy who will accompany me inside. I learned to distrust from so many past experiences. I was deceived and swindled. I am afraid that saying he is alive is just a ruse to take money from me. I do not want to put you in danger, but I, in the utmost sincerity, I do not trust anyone except you... and this trust does not force you to accept. You are free not to go.

I have never thought for once that a day may come where I would sit with Kabir khan in a public place for three hours while listening to his story as if I were watching a movie, astonished by the weird details of people's lives which I know nothing about. Maybe, Kabir khan's way of telling his story had something to do with me forgetting time, and who really was the person I was sitting with. Perhaps his story, and how honest he was, was the reason why I accepted to go with him to Syria.

***

The Cursed Heaven
…No one can imagine my mom was overwhelmed with happiness. When my younger sister was born after six males who filled the house with noise and chaos, my mother felt over the moon. In every pregnancy, she wished for a baby girl to help her with the affairs of the house and to feel safe with her when everyone else left the house and she started to feel lonely. Not surprisingly, my mother's overwhelming sense of loneliness with half a dozen boys was not something strange.

She was always telling us with a clear lance, "a day will come, and you all will leave as your elder brother did and will forget that you had a mother who carried you and took care of you." She was right in a big part of her sayings, but she had no right to think that we would abandon her and leave her to loneliness. Perhaps she purposely missed the idea of her daughter getting married and staying alone after that. Deep down inside, my mother was closer to solitude and contentment with how fate had designed her life. She believed in that innate way, which was not distorted by life experiences or reading, for she was illiterate. She inherited from her mother a great deal of beauty, which she passed on to half of the males and the other half bore my father's solid features and his pessimistic character. Maybe I am the only male who took his mother's beauty and his father's habits equally.

My mom named our sister Anjali, for she truly was a grace and joy in this life for us all… we were competing to take care of her, satisfy her, and teach her. None of us cared about the strict traditions imposed by our society that punished those who violate them. My mom was happy with the way we treated Anjali, but my dad was not. My father was a man committed to traditions and customs to the extent of sanctification, and he linked every tradition or habit with religion and attributed everything to Sunnah, threatening us with dire consequences in this world and the hereafter as punishment for our "infidelity". Every action we take must be on a specific scale, and if it deviates from it, it becomes infidelity.

The conflict between India and Pakistan did not appear in that fateful year, but for our family the beginning of the conflict started when my eldest brother was kidnapped from us. I was on the doorstep of youth when the news came at the end of the last millennium.

He was with one of the armed factions that crossed the Line of Control to the Kargil suburb in the Indian-administered sector of Kashmir.

When the coffin arrived, the habit of placing the body in a coffin was acquired in Pakistan after the violent events to cover the body, which was often mutilated. My father did not move; he remained in front of the door where he sat on an old couch, placed there for a rest under the shade of a mulberry tree. He sipped from a cup of red tea and called to my brother, who is five years older than me, to prevent my mother and sister from going out. This was according to our customary tradition of separating genders, to ensure that there was no communication, even in death cases. Reciting the Holy Quran and some religious poetic lines was a traditional activity during funerals. All the women in the family got involved in such an activity until the end of the funeral, after it was limited to my brother's wife.

My mom at that point had not grasped what was happening. My brother locked the door, men stayed to receive the coffin that we were not allowed to open, and we were ordered to take it to the cemetery immediately… one of the brothers commented: "The martyr should not be washed; burial is the way to honor the dead."

One of his companions whispered to my father: "He was a hero; you should be proud of him." I discovered that pride was a mysterious feeling; it was incomprehensible to me how one replaces one feeling with another! How can I let go of my sense of loss and bereavement to feel something I do not know what it is? My father rebuked me when he saw my tears: "Men do not cry." Another theory that I had to persuade, despite my certainty of its incorrectness and usefulness. Why don't men cry? Aren't they human beings, too?

Nevertheless, my father's phrase reinforced another feeling. It was my sense of masculinity and my responsibility for the family that my brother abandoned in order to escape from something I did not know.

I have never been alone with his wife, nor have I checked her features before that afternoon, which followed the passing of four months and ten days, during which she was forced to isolate herself in an inner room and she was prevented even from speaking!

Rajjo brought the tea and sat close to me and said:

"I need a favor from you, please do not let me down."

At that time, I noticed the glimpse of sadness that gathered the tears in her eyes and stopped the words in her throat. I encouraged her, avoiding looking in her eyes once again, for I felt something like a fire skewer pass through my heart. It was my sadness for losing my brother, for she was the live part of him… she begged with her voice, choking:

"Please ask your father, for me, to take the kids whilst I visit my mom for a few days." I was astonished by her request; was there any reason for me to intercede with my father in order for her to visit her family?

Out of love and respect, I promised her I would, and I did. Rajjo went to her parents' house and the days turned into weeks. At the beginning, I felt an overwhelming longing for the boys. With time, my feelings became clearer, and I missed Rajjo's presence. I honestly missed her place on the dining table, the tea she prepared and handed to me, and her presence in the kitchen. Her hair's smell after a shower… when my thinking reached this point, I felt that my heart almost stopped... was it possible that I liked her without knowing?

The question took another formula after a month of absence. "Do I love her?" No doubt I was a foolish boy. At that age, it was inconceivable that I fell in love with a woman who was older than me and had two children. Most importantly, that woman was my brother's wife!

One day, my dad surprised me:

"Didn't you think about getting married?"

"No, I will finish my university first. I hope to have a good job that will enable me to help you and help my sister get married. More importantly, I will take care of my brother's kids."

"Marriage will cost you nothing. The house is there, and the bride is from us."

I felt a trap would be applied to my soul; I wanted to marry a girl I loved. I was not going to marry in this way, but I did not want to anger my father who saw that protecting the kids required me to marry their mother. Besides, since she was a widow, things would be very easy. Her place in the house was preserved, and my mother got used to living with her and the children... it seemed that everything was agreed upon and considered by all parties, and nothing else left but my approval. Frankly, I had a hidden desire driving me to silence which made me justify my actions by the desire of others, not by my own.

At night, the two families agreed on the date of the marriage. I caught a glimpse of Rajjo's congested with blood face and her eyes filled with tears. She put the tea tray on the table in front of us and ran to the kitchen. Mom winked at me to follow her... but I did not move. It was obvious that Rajjo did not want to marry me… and I was sure of that when an old friend to my brother stopped me and asked me to talk privately. He in brief told me that he asked Rajjo to marry him before she got married to my brother and that they were in love, but her father refused that marriage because he wanted to marry her to a family that was wealthier and more sophisticated than his family… he told me that Rajjo was a victim, and after my brother's death they met and promised each other to get married again, but her father swore that this marriage wouldn't take place. Unusually, her father went far by firing him and threatening to accuse him of killing my brother if he tried to see Rajjo again... her father was right. I too began to suffer from doubts. Why did he go with the faction while he was not trained well on using weapons? Why did everyone go back on foot except for him? How would I allow someone who was accused of killing my brother to raise my brother's children? It was then that I convinced myself that my marriage should take place in order to eliminate a rumor that would shake our family if she married that man. Another reason was that I wanted to protect my brother's kids from living with a strange man.

We got married… but I could not get close to Rajjo. That night I slept on the floor while she slept in bed. The first few weeks passed, and my sense of estrangement and helplessness increased. Every time I got close to her; I saw the ghost of my brother getting in between us. To my surprise, she too never took off her black dress with long sleeves. She never talked to me, only fulfilled my requests while she looked at me unintentionally. I feel like her chest was loaded with hate towards me in every action she took. Finally, she made me think of running away.

The opportunity to be admitted to the university came as

a temporary solution to our problem.

The strange thing was that a few months after I traveled, I started receiving messages from Rajjo. It was Anjali who wrote it beautifully. This talented girl from her childhood was adept at writing, describing others and expressing their feelings, which made me fight for her to continue her study to the extent that satisfied her. Anjali was over thirteen years old... she told me that she avidly read my books and that she was learning sewing to please my mother, tricking my father into sending her to middle school, and exceptionally passed in elementary school. When I went back in the summer after I had finished my university, I was surprised by a girl wearing a sari standing in front of the door, sending her long hair in a huge braid that reached her right knee. I looked at her in astonishment... her beauty dazzled my eye. Was it possible that time had neglected me to this extent!? Anjali ran and hugged me shyly.

She stammered:

"My mom is sick; she could not wait for you here."

Me traveling to work in Afghanistan was harder on my mom than illness. She cried heartily:

"I am afraid you will not come back; I cannot handle another loss."

My mother was right, my older brother was killed and the next volunteered in the army was me. She was afraid that she would lose me, too. I was able to convince her that I was going to a safe place and that I was working with organizations, and I had nothing to do with the fight over there, but she did not stop crying:

"They kill everyone who disagrees with them, it does not matter who you are or where you come from."

My mother's ghost and her tears never stopped chasing me in nightmares that lasted my whole stay in Afghanistan… and when I decided to return, another heartbreaking news awaited me… my dad had gone during my absence. The woman, who feared loneliness, remained with her daughter, the widow of her son, and her two sons after my brothers had left to work and study in the capital. A house inhabited by women and ghosts celebrated my presence as if I were a mythical being who would save them from something unknown that squeezed their delicate hearts and fragile bodies.

I did not tell them that it was just a vacation, and that I was traveling to work in Turkey, until my travel time came.

My mom knew nothing about the country I was going to work in. When I explained to her about it and showed her pictures, she said with a smile:

"Was there no war there?"

"No, relax, a quiet and beautiful country. My job is easy, and the salary is good. Anjali will finish her study and I will pay her dowry and she will be the happiest bride in the whole province."

Perhaps it was the beautiful dreams that my mother had about her daughter's marriage that made her agree on my travel and pray for me to be satisfied.

I did not know this would be the last time I would see my mother, when she said goodbye in front of the door and her weak legs did not carry her until the car parked a few meters away.

A few months ago, I received an email from Anjali telling me that my mother could no longer get out of bed and that she invoked the spectrum of my brothers who had left the world and spoke with them and with my father day and night.

Therefore, she wanted me to travel to Syria to search for my youngest brother who went there for jihad and revenge for the blood of his two brothers. I did not tell you my middle brother was killed in Afghanistan. We did not discover that he had deceived us and told us lies that he had volunteered in the army until we got the news of his death. More sadly, they could not find his body. Just one of those who was fighting with him brought his stuff and gave it to my younger brother.

***

Kabir khan ignored talking about his relationship with Rajjo after he had come back from Afghanistan. I did not ask him what happened after that. I felt that he did not want to talk about her. That was why I preferred not to ask him.

The Lost Paradise

My agreeing to go with Kabir khan was an adventure with unknown results. Until the hour in which we got into the car on the way to the Bab al-Hawa crossing, I did not feel that I was taking an adventure. I even made sure to convince myself that I was on a quick visit to the country that still inhabited me, and that I missed everything in it and those who stayed in it.

On the Syrian side of the crossing, Abo Yusuf was waiting for us, standing next to a big blue Pickup worth for moving furniture. Its tires were huge and high. Kabir khan got in first and then helped me to get in. It was my first time in a semi-truck. The spacious interior provided a comfortable seating space and prevented from seeing the small things that might have stood in front of the front tires. When Abu Yusef sped up, it caused dust that prevented me from seeing and penetrated my chest. I was suffocating, and the cough did not help me get rid of its unpleasant effects... Kabir khan asked him to slow down and explained to us what we were going through on the road.

Abu Yusef was upset, that was clear in his tone, but he did not want to show hostility to a high-ranking foreign employee in the organization, and he was just a driver who brought aid and distributed it in the villages and cities we worked in.

The way he took after we had got out of Sarmada was a deserted country road. We only encountered a few people driving motorbikes while we were walking... we arrived at Taftanaz. Along the road occupied by the airport was a stone wall painted white. Writings in black paint occupied it, and some banners rested in front of it. The walls of the empty airport had turned into advertisements telling the reality of the situation in the area controlled by the armed factions. The most powerful of these signs was hadith attributed to the Messenger, may peace and blessings be upon him: "Tourism for my nation is jihad for the sake of God."

I translated to Kabir khan some of it as he asked me to. He wanted to understand the situation of the place in which the truck was quickly plundering its roads, as if it was racing to the finish line.

My heart pounded as I contemplated the Red Plains, the rich-with-blood-colored soil, the plant-free... the soil that gave wheat in our country its flavor and hardness, and which our grandmothers sifted when it was harvested while it was green, to grill it to become "freekeh", or leave it on its ears to dry and harvest it to make it "bulgur or flour for bread". The red plains nurse the olives of the governorate with its heir pure milk so that its oil shines and quenches the people's veins in health and wellness.

The road to Saraqeb did not take too long. The last time I saw the city was five years ago when I was in high school. The western neighborhood was our destination. I was looking at the frescoes and graffiti on the destroyed ceilings and walls… when I found this phrase that was not accompanied by color or image, it was satisfied with the whiteness of the wall and the blackness of the ink:

(You get forgotten as transient love, like a flower in the snow…you get forgotten. Know that you are free and alive when you get forgotten.)

I took a picture with my phone of it. Kabir khan asked me why and insisted to translate it to him… his eyes shone as I translated it into English... he whispered:

"It reminds me of our great poet Tagore."

I said with amazement:

"It did not come to my mind that you read poetry."

"One does not have to read for Tagore; he is the conscience of the Indian people. Even those who do not read know him as well as they know their Savior Gandhi."

"Mahmoud Darwish is the conscience of an entire nation – so to speak - it is better to say that his poetry is the conscience of a nation."

It seemed that the glimpse of smile that appeared in spite of me caught Kabir Khan's attention, and he understood that it was underestimating his saying. He stopped walking and said:

"It is not a proper time to discuss poetry, but someday I will give the complete works of Tagore as a gift, which he wrote in English. He will convince you, not me. I think we have reached our destination. But I do not see around me but destroyed houses! I do not think anyone lives here." The green vines laden with clusters of grapes and jasmine trellises behind the ruined walls, and houses without doors inviting the transients to enter, suggested that there was life in the inner rooms. I said:

"The address is correct; people are inside. It is the habit of the people of Saraqeb to leave the doors of their homes open during the day, and the fact that the door is broken and their clothes on the laundry rope indicates their presence."

I called out:

"People of the house."

Kabir khan laughed:

"This one, I know it."

A young man who looked in his early forties came out to us; I was shocked when I learned that he was not yet thirty!

He welcomed Kabir khan, shook his hands, and asked him to get inside. Without turning to me, he added:

"Perhaps it is more appropriate for the sister to enter the room where the women are sitting."

I said to Kabir khan:

"I will wait for you here; I do not want to enter."

The young man was embarrassed, and consequently said in confusion:

"I swear I did not mean to, I thought you wanted to."

"I did not know that about the people here that they separate women and men; it is more likely my idea was wrong."

"It is true to some point. I knew previously that you are coming with Kabir khan as a translator, but we can communicate with him without a translator."

I looked at Kabir khan. He said calmly:

"I prefer her to stay with me. I mean no offense, but my

English is not good enough. You will not understand it, she is used to my accent and understands it well."

The young man shook his head and seemed forced to agree.

Obviously, the conversation that took place between a group of young men and Kabir khan made me understand the reason for which they wanted me out. Not surprisingly, the looks of one of them were rude and were clearly mocking. I did not translate anything they said to Kabir khan. The young man who welcomed us did the job, and it was obvious he was the house owner, and he was the only one who did not put his weapon beside him.

When we went out, I breathed a sigh of relief and asked Kabir khan:

"What have you decided? Would you pay the amount they asked you to know where your brother was?"

He did not answer. Instead, he stepped away from me. I did not follow him. I remained numb on the sidewalk as the mortar shell left a wide hole... I moved the dirt with my feet in a circular motion, a small wave of dust struck, and the winds swept it up, slapped my face and teared my eyes. For a moment, the place vanished. I closed my eyes to a vast desert scene. Kabir khan was running into a whirlwind that threw him to the ground, rolling him over, his body curled into a huge egg that was blown by the wind and split in half.

Within minutes I lost my sense of time. Lina Shamamyan's voice reached me:

"The man with the brown skin has captivated my heart and his love has exhausted me. "

Fatigue is not what I was feeling, but a lump in the heart that I could not explain. The dust settled from Kabir Khan's face, standing before me:

"Are you hurt?"

"No."

"Your eyes are red. Are you sure that you are, okay?"

I did not know how to respond, because I did not know exactly how I felt. Bad? Okay? No doubt I was in the white area, just a void cut by an only true dot "hunger pinch". I said:

"I am hungry."

Kabir khan smiled for the first time since we arrived to Saraqep:

"Where do we go, you think? Do we mean the market?"

"The people in here do not know the simplest rules of etiquette; most dangerously, they lack what is called the common sense. They should invite us to stay for lunch. Do they not see that we are strangers and do not know how to move in the city?"

"But you know."

"Let's suppose I was not with you!"

"Let's go."

We ate a falafel sandwich, drank a cold cola, and Kabir khan called Abu Yusef to help us.

Abu Yusef was not late. Within minutes, his truck stopped near us in the middle of the market. I sat in the back seat and relaxed… the falafel meal was enough to make me sleepy. Abu Yusef asked:

"Where are you going?"

I said:

"We want a place to rest."

"The town as you know has no hotels, restaurants, or rest places. I can take you to a friend's place where you can rest and decide what you want to do."

"Won't we embarrass him?"

"He is not there, the house is empty, and luckily the key is with me. He gave it to displaced people from Ariha and they left a few days ago. The furnishings in the house are simple, yet sufficient."

Kabir khan agreed, and I for a short nap agreed as well. Abu Yusuf did not know what the relationship between me and Kabir khan might be. On the surface, it seemed that he was shy to ask, so I left him to think that we were together in order not to be embarrassed to leave us at his friend's house alone.

The house was a villa with two floors built with Syrian hard rocks. As usual, the rooms were wide, and the kitchen was big, overviewing a back garden full of olive trees and rose bushes which seemed to be watered by the neighbors. Abu Yusef warned us that the neighbors in the back villa had been annoyed by the presence of strangers in the villa and they did not want anyone to stand behind the windows, so they wouldn't see the women in their house. A smile struck my lips against my will, since when the residents of Saraqeb were fanatic, Abu Yusuf answered without me asking!

"It is not being strict. Don't you think they are ISIS? They are just relatives with the villa owners, and they do not like strangers. That is why the displaced who were living here left the place after they had a fight with them."

I promised Abu Yusuf to keep the windows shut and not to go out to the kitchen yard since we did not need it at all. I made a cup of coffee after I woke up from a nap that lasted for an hour and a half. I took a chair out and sat on the balcony that overlooked the street. Abu Yusuf left us a "talkie walkie". He said that people who lived here did not dispose of them. They used it to track the air traffic movement and also to replace the landline phones that were no longer working. Often there was no mobile phone coverage, in the light of the constant power outages for long hours, and we would not be able to use the WhatsApp service.

When we were alone, I asked Kabir khan:

"Have you made up your mind to give them a million liras? I think that it is a huge amount, then I have the feeling that they are swindlers."

"I will not pay until I see my brother. They have claimed that he is in the prisons of Al-Nusra Front in Ma'arrat al-Nu'man. They arrested him after a battle in which I do not know the two sides or where it happened, but they say that the front demands large sums of money for every person they release. The problem is not the money; I can afford the money and the amount the fixer asked for. The real question is, " do I trust that they will release him?"

I too doubted they would do. More suspiciously, the guy with the rude looks aroused suspicion in my heart further. I told Kabir khan I would not accompany him to Ma'arrat al-Nu'man in case he wanted to take the risk and pay them the money. I felt a real fear based not only on hunches, but on the knowledge of the morals of those who would accompany Kabir khan. If someone knew that he was not my husband, I would have no choice but to be arrested and stoned to death for adultery. I explained this to Kabir khan. He quickly said:

"For sure, I was not thinking about taking you with me. I know them very well. I saw people like them in Afghanistan."

I smiled:

"So, you are the guys who exported terrorists who dressed as jihadists and claimed to support Islam."

"You are wrong! America made them. America is the one

who created the right environment for them and released their hands to kill and implement their law to return people to the ages of darkness, to keep their grips on our necks. It is the iron fist of America with which to fight the bright minds of the Middle East."

I left Kabir khan sitting on the balcony, went to the room, locked the door, and laid on the bed. Uncomfortably, the bed was small and narrow. It seemed that it was one of the house owner's beds, but it was sufficient.

The hot weather was tempered by occasional gusts of air, although it was hot and pretty humid. Suddenly the ceiling fan moved, the electricity came! I was blessed with a nice hour, then evening came, and darkness fell after the sunset call to prayer. As a child, I was dazzled by the stars in the sky that I would watch when I slept on the roof of my grandfather's house. The house that is now rubble and nothing remains from its memory but a pile of stones, gesturing with sorrow to its beautiful past when it was protecting, concealing, and giving warmth in winter and preventing the heat in summer.

Faint clicks on the door and Kabir khan's voice woke me up:

"I made tea. Would you like to share it me with?"

I got up unwillingly. I swept my figure in front of a small mirror which topped the wardrobe. The fumes from the tea were refreshing. It was the first time Kabir khan had changed his habit:

"Weird! You did not make green tea as usual; do you have a stomachache?"

He smiled:

"No, but I only found red tea."

Kabir khan's habit - and it is his country's habit, as he told me - is to always drink green tea, and to use red tea only when he wants to cure a digestive problem. Which surprised me because we were doing the exact opposite. The origin is the red, and green tea is the exception.

"I will leave with Abu Yusuf at dawn. Can you bear staying here alone?"

"It's not scary, anyway. If I need something, I will knock on the neighbors' door."

"Did you not tell me that your relatives live here? "

"Their house is far in Tall Al Ruman. I cannot go there on foot, or I even do not want to go. Curiosity will prompt them to investigate and find out why I am here and with whom I came. I do not want to tell anyone about it."

"You are right. I will try to come back quickly."

***

Abyss's edge
Kabir khan did not wake me up at dawn, and I did not hear the sound of steps or a car. In the morning, when the western breeze stopped, and the sharp annoying rays of sun started penetrating the window glass, I got up from bed, sweating. I needed a few minutes to comprehend where I was. I looked in the small mirror. My face was puffy as usual, but this time tarnished by ugly red dots left by raging bugs and midges at night.

Summer days are often long and annoying, especially in the light of the electricity cuts and the quiet air. I used to put a book in my back bag so that reading could help me get rid of my sense of boredom. I searched for the book, but I could not find it. My sense of malaise increased, and I felt almost suffocated... I made a cup of tea and ate some fruits. There was a closed room, but its key was hanged with a nail above the door, which suggested that the owners of the house placed their furniture that they did not want the visitors to use in it and did not take the key in case of emergencies. I hesitated a lot in opening the door. I overcame my hesitation by convincing myself that it was a case of emergency. My guess was correct; they had a humble library but most of the books were in law and medicine. There were also many books about the interpretation of the Holy Qura'an, an only book in dream explanation, and a part of 'The Story of Civilization' with the cultural center stamp on it. The variety of the books showed that the house owner had borrowed some of them and could not find time to give them back. Luckily, I finally found something to read.

I did not know the importance of this book, and it never crossed my mind to go through it before. When my grandfather's library was within my reach, he beautifully placed the bound parts of this book in the middle, surrounded by the works of Tolstoy and Chekhov. I used to think that it was a boring book that adults would boast about reading in order to suggest to those around them that they were highly educated and wise... Its parts were up to fifty parts, as I remember its yellow leaves were alienating me. I did not like to read big books, especially with yellow pages. I feel comfortable reading a novel printed on smooth white satin paper. And that is what made me stay away from my grandfather's library contents and look for the books I wanted to read somewhere else.

Maybe I am lucky for the part in my hands talking about India. It was a chance to know better about the nature and history of the country where Kabir khan came from and whether it was written with the view of a foreign writer.

Barely had I finished the first hundred pages when I heard the tire sound of a car stopping in front of the door. I got up, peering from the balcony, and saw Kabir khan getting off Abu Yusuf's truck and asking him to wait. When Kabir khan saw me, he said:

"Bring your bag and come, we are leaving."

Kabir khan asked me before the truck left Saraqeb:

"Are you hungry?"

I understood that he had been himself hungry; it was a way to express what he wanted… I did not answer. I asked Abu Yusuf to stop in the market in order that we could buy some pies and fruits. I did not ask Kabir khan what happened in Al Ma'ara. It was obvious from his facial gestures that he did not get the chance to see his brother.

When we reached the crossing boundaries from the Syrian side, Abu Yusef bade farewell and wished us to arrive safely and told me:

"God willing, good news will reach him within weeks. I will pursue the matter until I know where his brother is."

Abu Yusuf did not lie. After two weeks I received a message from him saying, "It was more likely that Kabir khan's brother had been in the prisons of ISIS in Raqqa city. I am not sure yet of the news, but one of my relatives at the front told me that Jund al-Aqsa arrested him during clashes with the front, then they exchanged him for ISIS detainees in Raqqa. Tell him not to risk coming. It is not safe here for someone like him. Last time, he miraculously ran out of their hands… but who knows if they know about him being here."

The message worried me. Why had Kabir khan not told

me what had happened with him in Al Ma'ara?

I confronted him with anger:

"What happened there?"

He raised his head from the computer screen, surprised by my accent:

"There! Where? What is it with you?"

"What happened in Al Ma'ara?"

"It is not appropriate to tell you, I do not want to bother you."

Not because of my insistence, Kabir khan suddenly collapsed and got up to the bathroom. He needed a long time to tell me:

"If Abu Yusef had not been with me, I would have been in awe. They handcuffed me and threw me blindfolded in a closed room. They took my money and luckily, I left my personal papers in the car with Abu Yusuf. When I was late, he followed me to the headquarter. They were at that moment alerted due to a sudden clash on the outskirts of the town near the cemetery because of the funeral of a martyr from the Free Army. Abu Youssef released my handcuff after he deported the person assigned to guard me. He was driving the truck like a maniac who did not leave us all the way until we got there. Honestly, I was afraid of implicating you more so; I decided to go back, but I would not stop searching for him. My mother is asking me daily about him and she thinks I have the power to bring him back in the job I occupy."

Four months have passed since that incident, and my relationship with Kabir khan has become very formal during that period. I was working silently and contented with sending the work by email. Even the morning greeting I said without looking at him.

Early December, he surprised me with a strange request:
"Can I invite you to the café to have a cup of coffee?"
"What is the occasion?"
"You will know if you accept my invitation."

Once again, was it curiosity or something else that prompted me to accept the invitation? I did not regret the time I spent with Kabir khan in Meclis... for the first time, Kabir Khan did not babble with his strange accent, but rather he summarized what he had wanted to say in short, quick sentences:

"I want to say goodbye to you. I will go to Syria in a last attempt to see my brother before the organization closes its doors and I move to Iraq."

The decision of closing the organization in a month depressed me. Therefore, I would again enter the job search whirlpool. After I had lost the chance to go by sea to Europe, I did not know which demon made me say:

"I will go with you."

Kabir khan opened his mouth in astonishment and said nothing. He stared at my face for so long that I turned away mine from him, contemplating the shallow waters of the river. I did not want to retreat from my decision that I had already made without thinking. With great efforts on my behalf, I tried to know why but I could not. I told myself, "let it be. Sometimes the decisions we make arbitrarily prove to be the right ones."

I asked him:

"Are you going to go to Raqqa?"

"No, I was told that he is now fighting with Jund al-Aqsa while he is in a village near Sarmin that I do not know its name. Maybe Al-Nayrab, is there a village with this name?"

"Yes, there is that can be near Saraqep. Do not bother if he is there, because going there is very easy."

***

Nancy Storm
At that time, the weather was so cold, the mountain peaks around Atma bleached from the accumulated snow. The road Abu Yusef took was slippery because of the mud that the agricultural machinery left on the asphalt and melting snow. The vision was almost not clear; that was why Abu Yusef drove the truck cautiously, which made us need double the time to reach Saraqeb. This time, Abu Yusef prepared a room for us in the house of a friend of his in the Western neighborhood, opposite Al-Shifa Hospital... I did not know if it was mere coincidence, for I knew the house very well, and I knew its owners. I remembered that once in my childhood I had visited it with my father. At that time the house was very different, its walls were more beautiful. Furthermore, the courtyard of the house was filled with rose pots, grapes and jasmine larches, and the warm night and the echo of distant laughter accompanied the whistling sound of the teapot on the fire. Was that time really gone and not going back?

The house looked deserted and disoriented despite the fact that the furniture that overcrowded the room was attached to the roof "attic" and the fireplace that raged with fire.

I was standing at the window watching the empty narrow street in the afternoon when I saw an ambulance stop in front of the hospital door. Two paramedics got out from it, opened the back door, and they put down two bodies, apparently of two women, who had an accident. I expected it to be a car accident. Today was calm, I did not hear the sound of shelling or a plane. A few minutes passed before the ambulance left and a group of women gathered in front of the outside door. Besides, quarrel sounds came from the end of the street. Maybe it was from the main street… I checked the clock was five p.m. Kabir khan had not come back yet! He told me he would not be late. I was too anxious to know what had happened. Anxiety made me wear my coat, put my hair under my beanie and put a thick colored scarf above that covered my eyes, and go downstairs. I opened the door. The western wind was so strong, about to uproot my body and throw it away. I approached the women and asked one of them in a whisper: "Is it an accident?" She stared at me in amazement: "It seems you are a stranger; it is better not to appear in the street with these clothes on." Suddenly, she pulled me by my hand, brought me back to the house entrance and said:

"They may come now. You should not get out of the house. Is Abu Yusuf your relative?"

"Yes."

The woman smiled:

"Are you married?"

"Yes."

" Better, is your husband with you?"

"Yes."

The woman's questions did not stop flowing over my head until I repeated my question about the accident and invited her to enter in order not to stay in the cold. I poured her a cup of tea; she sat cross-legged by the stove and brought her hands close to it until she almost hugged it… she asked me where my husband was working and what I was doing here. I stopped her and repeated my question for the third time. She seemed upset, but she answered:

"Allah's law applied to them."

I did not understand what she had meant. When she saw me surprised, she added,

"The punishment of adultery, you know, is stoning to death."

I was about to shout, who are they? Who gave them the right? How did that happen? The woman looked away and wiped her tears with the sleeve of her robe and said:

"God granted them the right, and this is his judgment, but I am sure that they are innocent. I've known them since my childhood, some of their male relatives were upset with them for not getting married. One of them inherited a big olive land and the other one inherited two houses from their father… those who covet their money are many, and rumors about them are more. The legitimate committee does not need evidence, as it is imposed in Islam they suffice with the statements of false witnesses. I am sure that the one who carried out the stoning knows with certainty that they are innocent of the charge. However, the flock always walks behind the dog, may God bless you.

I repeated the phrase behind her while distraught. Before she asked permission to go, I had heard the truck stop in front of the door. The woman greeted Kabir khan and went out. I could not explain his features. His body was trembling, he got close to the stove, took the teapot, poured one glass of tea, and sat on a chair near the window. I waited for him to tell me what happened. He said:

"It was horrible, I saw him pointing the gun into their heads and pushing them with his feet to a deep hole… I saw him with my own eyes… I could not get close, I wanted to call out for him, I wanted to tell him, "do not kill Anjali", but words stopped in my throat. I totally shut up... is it possible that my brother was killing brutally? What can I say to my mother? Your son is killing the people here, do not worry on a murderer, do not pray for his victory rather for guidance... your son is killing in the name of religion you raised him on. This is your upbringing. No, it is not hers, my mom could not give birth to a killer... but she has given birth to all. The three of my brothers chose Jihad, the three of them choose to be murderers... what can I say to her? Tell me...

I too was silent, what can I say to him? I saw the two women. I saw shredded clothes, blood, and deformed features, I did not see the two women. Should I tell him that his crime is mitigated because he was not alone? There was a group of men who lost their humanity and mind and obeyed the orders of their prince. No, not possible, he was fully responsible for his actions... I will not justify him for what he has done.

"When are we going back?"

"Now if you want. Abu Yusuf is ready to take us to the crossing."

The car lost its balance when we arrived to Taftanaz plains because of the winds. Abu Yusef stopped it passing the airport wall:

"I cannot go on until the rain stops."

Abu Yusuf was right; the storm was severe, and he could not adventure driving the car in rain that blocked one meter of vision. I took a book out of my bag. Kabir khan asked me:

"You are reading for Khaled Hosseini?"

"Yes, I do not like translated books. That is why I often read the English version. It is a gift from a friend. Do you want to borrow it?"

"No, I read it before you. Isn't it a weird coincidence?"

"Which coincidence?"

"Marie's death in the novel and what I saw today. I saw the stoning scene in an Iranian movie. When the film ended, I thought deeply, "it is just a movie." You will not be sad and confuse your life for a movie. The heroin well get up, shake off the dirt, and wipe off that red liquid. She will bathe and wear elegant clothes and will go to celebrate her success in the role and will forget everything related to that woman who was actually stoned… it is just acting… a glass, a smile and an invitation to dinner from her lover or husband. She will forget all that she has endured to master the role. The whole time I watched, I waited for the two women to finally get up, wipe the mud and blood off their faces, get into the car and return to their home."

"We cannot fool ourselves in this way, what you saw today was extremely brutal."

Abu Yusuf smiled and said:

"The brutal incidents in the recent period are countless. Since Al-Nusra Front entered the region, life has been going backwards. Today's stoning incident is no more brutal than the killing of Sajah and her sister."

"Sajah! Do you mean the nurse?"

"Do you know her?"

"I remember her from when I was a little kid. She is my father's relative, a 'Distant one', but I remember her very well from when she injected me with a needle against a disease. I cannot remember what it was, I remember only that she was fast and light. The pain the injection caused was not as much as the fear and terror that afflicted me. Her smile lingered in my memory attached to the purple candy she gave me saying that it removes the pain quickly! She was a very old woman, what was her charge?"

"Mystery still surrounds their deaths, there is not much detail, but one of the Mujahideen who drove them from the house to the prison told me about the details… no doubt you know a lot about her since she is your father's relative."

Yes, I heard them talking about her, strange tales that to me were just myths and the gossip of ignorant women. But now that Abu Yusuf told the story, everything was clear.

(Hajj Abd al-Hay did not have males. Life gave him two daughters, and their mother died before the eldest Sajah became ten years old. That was the year of famine. No one knows the exact date of Sajah's birth, as she was from those who did not have a formal record. Her father registered her in the personal status department when he wanted to send her to school to receive an education when he saw signs of ingenuity and an interest in books… at the age of thirty, she enrolled in nursing school and returned to work in a doctor's office in town. Then she worked for a while in the infirmary and retired when her father passed away at the age of more than one hundred years old and took his place at the age of fifty.

Before the death of her father, Sajah did not work in writing "veiled", and it never occurred to her to open one of those yellow books that her father's "library" contained. But when Sheikh Abdel Hay approached to die, he taught Sajah everything related to his profession that he had practiced for sixty years. Before that, he was an imam of a mosque who followed one of the Sufi orders and retired in a corner of his own for more than ten years. He was intended by men and women to solve their earthy problems. Then he found himself practicing writing veils and was a specialist in removing magic, deciphering knots and reconciling hearts. He never in his life has harmed anyone and he strongly refused to write black magic to anyone, even though he was good at it.

In the beginning, Sajah's work was limited to treating sick women and children by reading the Qur'an and using herbs. Then she dared to write the veils, and she became famous in the neighboring villages, and her customers increased.

That was in the late eighties when she started receiving men as well... no one condemned her work, on the contrary, most people believed that she was the successor to Sheikh Mubarak Abdul-Hay, and she was not classified as a woman. Her nickname was Sheikha Sajah, and her name was unambiguous, but most of those who knew her thought that they were talking to Sheikh Abdul-Hay, for Sajah had a rough voice that did not belong to femininity, and she used to wear her father's cloak over her clothes and cover her head with the sugar-colored shawl that he used to put on his fez. She did not change the room that people had gotten used to, nor the incense ritual, and her father's room remained with that special scent of him, the scent of Arabian musk.

Sajah grew old and aged, but she only stopped working for a short time when she suffered a slight stroke that left its mark on her legs, and they were paralyzed... her younger sister's luck was not better than hers with men, as she got married at the age of thirty to a man twenty years older than her. He divorced her a year later when she did not give birth as he wanted. So she returned to her father's house to help her sister in the household affairs. She was not showing up in Sajah's room, nor were any of the customers seeing her, nor was her voice heard. She carried out cleaning, cooking and buying household necessities silently and quietly… then she learned nursing from her sister and took care of her after her illness… she bought her a wheelchair so that she could take her out for a weekly walk, scouring the fields on the outskirts of town at afternoon and returning in the evening. After the outbreak of the revolution, people almost forgot Sajah. Some thought she was dead. Everybody was surprised when they saw armed men knocking the door and bringing her out carried, and behind her, her sister shouting, crying, and begging them to let her come with her because she needed the medicine at specific times and needed someone to feed her, because she could not eat alone.

The huge gunman put Sajah on the ground and waited for her sister, who brought the chair, the medicine bag, and the blanket to wrap her helpless sister's legs.

The whisper that roamed the town from east to west was just guessing and speculation about the reason for which they arrested Sajah, and about the place they took her to… Sajah was absent from the town for three months, and no one asked about her… have people lost their curiosity? It was not due to the lack of curiosity, but to the many misfortunes, deaths, and destruction. Sajah's story no longer aroused anyone's curiosity until people saw her and her sister's bodies lying in front of their house door.

Sajah's accusation was her usage of sorcery, perhaps her name, which she carried, stirred in the hearts of the men of the body that sentenced her to death, the memory of the woman who claimed prophethood and lover by the liar Musailimah, even though it was said that she died following the religion of Islam… but what everyone did not understand was why they executed Radah when she was not even wanted and accompanied her sister just to take care of her.

Some have said that Radah's silence about her sister's crimes and her practice of witchcraft and sorcery is also a crime, and she was not killed directly, but was judged by the men of the Commission and was found guilty, for she could not live with her sister under one roof for all those years without her soul absorbing the black magic that her sister spread with the help of demons in the house. Some women went so far as to explain that Sajah had been married to an infidel genie all her life and that her sister knew about it and was covering her up… so, the two deserved the punishment inflicted on them.

No one knows who buried the bodies of the two women, nor where their tombs are. The sheikhs in the country considered that the two women, as they are proven, are infidels, and it is not permissible to bury them in the town cemetery. But everyone knows, even if they do not say it publicly, who poured oil around their house and set it on fire. For fear has returned to re-inhabit hearts in a new way.)

The storm had not calmed down and the o'clock had passed five, which was the time for the crossing to be closed… we had to seek refuge in a camp near Sarmada, which consisted of several simple random buildings. It was built with modest resources for young men working in the area. The room was crowded with men and the thick smoke from cigarettes was making the place suffocating. Abu Yusuf said:

"You can relax in the kitchen."

The statement was frank; I could not sit with men. It was an appropriate solution until the weather improved, but the issue was no longer linked to the weather for the morning…

not only was it stressful, but it was also embarrassing. How am I going to spend the night here? I called Abu Youssef to find a solution to the problem. He found it quickly. He accompanied me to a family home near the camp and asked them to host me until the morning.

Curious women surrounded me with questions. I did not find an escape except to close my eyes and make my head automatically fall on my chest to fall asleep while I was sitting. Then they pitied me and brought me a pillow and a blanket and left the room.

That was the last time I entered Syria… and the last time I met Kabir khan for a long time. Days after our return, the organization closed its doors, and Kabir khan traveled to Erbil, and I no longer heard anything from him.

***

Trauma

The memories that surprised me when I saw Kabir khan in his elegant clothes and pale face told me what was behind his calm and gloomy appearance... what I remember is that nothing could stop Kabir khan's passion and anger and fill him with sadness like this, except death. He definitely lost someone dear to his heart, but I did not want to know anything, since a long time ago I lost my desire to share with others their grief. Rather, I no longer concerned anyone's grief after the accumulation of sadness in my heart to the point of bereavement, and then I turned it into stifling ashes that eliminated my feelings entirely so I could read news of death as I read news of the exchange rate of the lira, or the latest fashion trends and news of artists, and the scene of the displaced in the tents became parallel to any scene from a movie that I saw on Netflix or YouTube. However, after we drank coffee, and a deep silence fell amid the airport noise, my curiosity suddenly erupted, and I do not know how I asked Kabir khan why he was here in Gaziantep after he had moved to Erbil.

"Are you here for work or a visit?"

"Neither this nor the other... I am here to take my brother's body."

Although I expected the reason for Kabir khan's presence to be strong and tragic, not to this extent. I understood that the death that kidnapped his brother this time was neither merciful nor tranquil as every person wishes to end on this earth. And it was not the first time that death experienced Kabir khan's tenacity and his attachment to a life that did not give him joy, even when it gave him the money he sought from his work with organizations in conflict areas, whether in Iraq or Syria, and before that in Afghanistan.

"Are you going to take him back to Pakistan?"

"No, it is done. I buried him here, and in a few hours, I will be back in Erbil. And you?"

Do I have to answer his question? I do not find it necessary for Kabir khan to know anything personal about me. The time distance that separates us is large and cannot be shortened in a passing and short conversation. I do not like for the conversation to diverge and become deep so that one of us does not have a desire for another meeting or a new kind of communication. It seemed that Kabir khan understood my silence or guessed it positively, so he asked for my phone number. I did not find it avoidable not to give him my number to prevent the embarrassment that we would fall into if I refused, and I considered the matter a compromise solution that in principle avoided me engaging in private conversations.

"Are you not married yet?"

The question surprised me, though it was a normal question that anyone may ask after a very long time. I answered briefly:

"No."

The severe shortening made Kabir khan shrink in his place, and his features expressed distress, but he soon gained control of his tension and said calmly:

"I expected that."

"On what basis?"

"Girls like you; they do not look for stability and cannot commit to a family life."

What Kabir khan said was true, but it bothered me that he had a deep knowledge in my personality. All those years I used to think that I was the invisible girl that others did not see when they passed by, did not get anyone's attention, and no one wanted, especially those whom she loved passionately, and really wished that someone would like to be in relationship with her. What happened was that none of them thought about being with me, and this is what made me tough and resistant later on to anyone trying to approach me in any way or form. I did not care about the description that others adopted of my personality, nor did I care about the assumptions that their imaginations had ignited with, to the point of saying that I am a lesbian. Everything that is rumored, and I hear touches my ears and sinks into the dark well. My heart is no longer beating with anything because of the large number of bodies, pictures and ashes of entire cities fallen into it. Suddenly I remembered Rajjo. I do not know what made her sit next to me in a chair on which I put my coat and bag. She smiled and asked kindly to pick up my things so she could sit down, for she was so tired from traveling. I almost believed my hallucinations reaching out to raise my coat. I heard Kabir khan asking me:

"You are looking for something? Cigarette box is in front of you."

"Ah, sorry, I did not see it… by the way, how is Rajjo?"

"Did I not tell you since we were in Antakya that I divorced her and married her ex-lover!?"

He certainly did not tell me. I wanted to satiate my curiosity with more nuanced details about his relationship with her, but I restrained myself because that would have made me seem interested in him and that was not true.

The question that I did not want to ask Kabir khan at the beginning of our conversation suddenly erupted against my will:

"Did you not marry after that?"

"No, I am still waiting."

"What?"

"A girl I loved five years ago, still waiting for her heart to open and see the truth in front of her."

"Which truth?"

"That I cannot love someone else, and I cannot marry but her."

He surprised me with a question:

"Still painting? I loved your painting about the Mevlevi, I wish you could have given it to me at that time."

"No, I am not sure that I paint well. I almost did not hold a brush since I left Antakya. It was not easy to bring my drawing tools to Istanbul, and I cannot buy others. It is so expensive; I do not have enough to practice that luxury."

"Painting is not a luxury; I think for you it is more important than food and drink."

"Sometimes I feel it is that important, for it helps to empty negative energy from my body and soul... but..."

I stopped suddenly, asked myself, what is pushing me to chat so simply with Kabir Khan? Since when did he care about my stuff?

"Why did you stop? Is there something bothering you? By the way, you look so beautiful."

My hand trembled. What did he say? He continued, embarrassed:

"Since I saw you, I noticed that something has changed in you. I do not know exactly what it is."

In fact, he knows very clearly that I have had my nose done, which has accompanied me for many years, my complex since my friend Tasnim pushed me at school and knocked me down on the pavement and broke my nose. Since that incident and I have been short of breath. The doctor advised me not to do a surgical operation until I was over eighteen years old. After my displacement, I did not have enough money to do the surgery... so, I postponed it until last year.

***

I was on my way to the plane gate when I got a WhatsApp message. The number that appeared on the screen was not in my contact list.

The message was long:

(I did not tell you, and maybe you do not want to know, but I need someone to share my pain with... on the 26th of February, clashes between Indian and Pakistan forces took place. The two sides exchanged fire shooting along the Line of Control... a number of citizens were killed. Among them, there was a woman and her child. That woman was Rajjo and my nephew).

The plane was about to take off when I received another notification. A second message saying:

(The girl I waited for, for five years was you.)

Kabir khan.

***

After Trauma

I shut my cellphone and put it in my bag. The tingling in the lower chest moved to my throat. I began to feel it shattering and thick dust gathering in it. I wanted to cough but I could not. I tried to get out of my stomach all the distress that accumulated on a long exhalation, and I failed... I grabbed a magazine and started checking it. I tried to hide my face with it when I saw Rima entering the plane! What foolish coincidence did bring her?

I have not met Rima since a while now, and I hate to meet her for she speaks a lot. She is never bored of bringing back the past and mocking everything that happened.

Rima is the daughter of a well-known lawyer in the governorate. Her house is on Al-jala'a Street, the street from which the Khansa'a School overlooks the garden on the opposite side. The city center is inhabited by rich people from ancient Idlib families.

She always talked about her grandfather, the Pasha, his properties, her Damascene mother, and her beauty and origins that struck the Ottoman Turkish depth. Although most of her friends know her Roman origins, for she comes from the Al-Bara town, this is clear from her surname.

I raised the magazine to my face in a way she could not see me when she passed by me. I heard her voice:

"Excuse me, my seat is the one beside you near the window."

My heart trembled as I slowly turned, half-turning, until our eyes met. I had to get up and make way for her to get into her seat. She put her bag in the cabinet above. I went in, trying to control my confusion, and to show my indifference as if I did not know her.

Before I sat, she looked at me while taking her sun glasses off her eyes with amazement:

"Unbelievable…"

She wanted to get up and hug me in the moment, I sat down and gave her a cold hand to shake. I leaned my head against the seat, suggesting an end to the conversation. The plane moved, I closed my eyes while I settled in the sky, and the passengers began loosening their belts, moving, and making noise.

Her palm touched my hand on the side bolster:

"Are you tired? So happy to see you. I love always to have a traveling companion to talk to him, to kill my boredom of waiting for the flight to end and land at the airport."

I nodded my head and said nothing. She added:

"You know? I hate flying, but I found traveling by plane is the most effective way. The distances between cities in Turkey are vast and the bus ride is cumbersome and takes a long time."

I knew that Rima had a phobia of flying and this was one of the reasons why I was so bothered about her being with me, for she wouldn't stop talking the whole time, and it would exhaust me to hear her follies and lies. I usually sleep when the plane takes off and wake up when it lands. I don't burden myself with flying problems, especially when the weather is bad, and it is known that most of the time the weather is bad. The plane has pitfalls, and the passengers are frightened… all these things I do not see nor feel…

"The coffee in the plane is bad. I like it heavy, and I like to flip my cup, even if there is no one to read it for me. By the way, do you still read cups? You know the last time you read my cup, it was all true, and most of it happened to me. I wanted to tell you before, and when I called a stranger picked up and said that he had newly bought the number and that he did not know who you are."

"I do not remember, when did I read the cup for you?"

"Last time we met in Istanbul at Arada restaurant, you really do not remember! That day you called me and said you are waiting for me at Aradas restaurant, and I asked you not to drink coffee until I arrived."

"Ah… I remember now. Farah was the one who called you, not me."

"Farah! Who is Farah? I do not know a friend with that name, and then we did not have a third person that day. It was just you and me."

Impossible, what was she saying? Farah was with us, Nariman's sister. I wanted to remind Rima of Farah. No doubt she had started to forget a lot. Before the words came out of my mouth, I receded… I thought for a bit, "what if…?" I choked with letters… Rima continued:

"Maybe you forgot, and you are talking about another meeting with another friend… I told you then that I do not love this restaurant and I prefer to go to Mado because I love the Armenian waitress who is working there."

"What? What is Rima saying? Is her memory weakened to this extent? The Armenian waitress works at Arada. I wanted to escape the talking to sleep, closed my eyes, but Rima did not stop chatting, and poked me in the shoulder:

"How can you sleep amid this noise? I really envy you, you have so many things I wish I can get. First off is boldness. Do you remember the demonstration we went to at the first of what you call 'revolution'?"

"Yes, I remember."

I muttered in a hushed voice. I did not want to oppose Rima, nor to discuss her. Perhaps she would let me relax until we arrived, but she insisted on continuing the conversation.

"That day I liked you and we became friends, although I hate what you call a revolution. From the beginning, I knew we would end up to diaspora. You would not bring down the regime. All that happened was that we lost our land and our homes and were displaced… wasn't it better for you now to be a college graduate? And your father who lost his land, it was the most beautiful olive land in the governorate. I never forget the distinctive taste of its oil… you know, sometimes it comes to my mind that if you had not slapped the officer's daughter that day, you would not have lost your land… I know how greedy he was and how provocative his daughter is. It is true that I was not with the revolution, and I used to befriend her for the sake of her father's authority, for that I was really happy… you broke her thorn and slathered her nose with dirt... did your father think that a five hundred olive oil tank would satisfy her father and make him pardon you? His daughter was provoking him to kill you. Maybe you would be dead by now if you had not fled to Turkey at the right time. Look at what the alleged revolution did... it has displaced, killed, destroyed and forsaken millions... and your father's land was lost with its olives, its trees uprooted, and used as firewood for heating... those Islamists who fought in your name and the name of your revolution."

I wanted to shout at Rima, "shut up". I knew the way she thought about the revolution, but what I could not endure was the obvious stupidity and confusion in her conversation, and what I could not bear most was what she was saying about me! That stupid liar, how could she attribute to me what Farah did? My father never begged the officer and did not give him the oil season to let me go. Did my father even have an olive grove?

"Shut up", I whispered. The noise of the plane covered my whisper... Rima's lips moved, continuing to chatter with her eternal stupidity, but her voice did not reach my ear. Had I lost my hearing? Voices exploded in my head suddenly...

The noise of the plane came back... and I heard Rima's voice:

"It seems you are in need for something to refresh your memory more. I will tell you an incident of you and I. If you remember it, I will be wrong and owe you an apology. If you do not, I advise you to see a psychologist. I do not accuse you of anything - God forbid - we all need a psychiatrist... we all suffer from the devastating effects of war... you are especially the ones affected the most, you lost many of your family under bombing..."

I interrupted her:

"Regime forces bombed. My relatives were buried under the rubble of their homes after barrel bombs fell on them. My brothers are in detention, and my grandmother is still trying to live with the ghosts of my uncles whom she lost successively... and you are telling me stupid stories about gunmen uprooting olive trees from my father's land. Who told you my father had an olive land?"

The pilot's voice announcing our arrival to Gazi Antep Airport silenced Rima... we fastened the belts and put the seats back upright. I closed my bag, checked my mobile phone and unlocked it...

"Won't you give me your new number?"

She did not wait. Rima snatched my phone from my hand and tried to open it. It did not respond. I smiled:

"It has a password... I will give you the number."

She sent me a test message from her number, and she said:

"We will continue talking via WhatsApp... if you are staying for long in Gazi Antep, let us meet for a coffee, and read the cup for me like old days."

The first message was from Rima, the one I thought was a test. She wrote: "for sure you will remember when you told me about the soldier who was wearing black, the one who came out from the egg!"

I did not arrive at the hotel and rest my body on the bed until Rima's messages poured out like stones over my head, and I could no longer distinguish which of us was right.

"No doubt you will be bothered by my messages, but you know that I am very frank. What do you think of visiting you in the hotel and talking? I know you will refuse, because of